GREAT ILLUSTRATED CLASSICS

THE HOUSE OF THE SEVEN GABLES

Nathaniel Hawthorne

Adapted by
Malvina G. Vogel
Illustrations by Pablo Marcos

BARONET BOOKS, New York, New York

GREAT ILLUSTRATED CLASSICS

edited by
Rochelle Larkin

Published by Playmore Inc., Publishers
230 Fifth Avenue, New York, N.Y. 10001
and Waldman Publishing Corp.
570 Seventh Avenue, New York, N.Y. 10018

Printed in the United States of America

Contents

About the Author

Nathaniel Hawthorne was born in 1804 in Salem, Massachusetts.

As a child, Nathaniel couldn't enjoy sports because of a slight limp, so he spent his time reading. His interest in literature at this early age greatly influenced his decision to become a writer as an adult.

Hawthorne studied at Bowdoin College in Maine. After graduation, Hawthorne returned to Salem where he spent the next twelve years improving his writing skills and in 1837 published a collection of short stories, *Twice-Told Tales.*

In 1842, Hawthorne married Sophia Peabody and they had three children. Since income from his writing was not enough to support his family, Hawthorne worked at the Boston Customs House, but still continued to write.

In 1850, Hawthorne published his first novel, *The Scarlet Letter*, which was an immediate success. When he began to write *The House of the Seven Gables*, he chose as his main theme the way a family's past can influence its descendants down through the years.

In 1852, Hawthorne published his third successful novel, *The Blithedale Romance*. With three successful novels in three years, Nathaniel Hawthorne had become an important writer. President Franklin Pierce appointed Hawthorne U.S. Consul in England. While there, Hawthorne traveled throughout Europe and gathered material for future novels and short stories, but none were as successful as his first three works.

Hawthorne died on May 19, 1864. He is still regarded as one of the leading figures in American literature. He influenced many writers who came after him.

The House of the Seven Gables

CHAPTER 1

The Old Pyncheon Family

For two hundred years, the old wooden house stood on a side street in a coastal New England town. The house was unusual; it had seven gables that extended in seven directions. So it was called The House of the Seven Gables. Some called it Pyncheon House.

A large elm tree had been growing for one hundred of those two hundred years between the front door and the street. The Pyncheon Elm, Pyncheon Street and Pyncheon House were all named for the Pyncheon family who had built the house and had been living there for two centuries.

A short history of the house and the

Pyncheon family will help to explain what happened before this story actually begins. It is a history of deception, of scheming... and of murder!

Pyncheon Street was once called Maule's Lane, and the land where The House of the Seven Gables now stands was once owned by Matthew Maule, who had built his log hut on the two acres. Originally the land was far from the center of town and had a fresh, clear spring of water on it. As years passed, the town spread out and reached Maule's land.

It was then that a well-known, wealthy and powerful man in the county, Colonel Pyncheon, became interested in the Maule property. He claimed that it was his, that it was part of a larger parcel of land that the government had given to him. It was the custom in colonial times for important, wealthy people with political connections to be given large land grants by the king.

Matthew Maule was a nobody; he was even considered a rather strange man. But when it came to defending his land, he was

Colonel Pyncheon Became Interested.

fierce in his refusal to give it up.

Unfortunately, people with wealth and power sometimes influence legal decisions. So when certain well-known people, including Colonel Pyncheon, were anxious to rid the town of people they believed to be witches and wizards, they targeted Matthew Maule. He was tried and found guilty of practicing witchcraft during the town's famous witch trials of the 1690s. Maule's sentence was death by hanging.

On the day set for the execution, Colonel Pyncheon sat on his horse watching the prisoner being led up to the scaffold. As the hangman put the noose around Maule's neck, the prisoner looked over at the colonel and cursed him, crying out, "God will give him and his descendants blood to drink!"

After Maule's death, Colonel Pyncheon took the land and decided to build his family mansion on the very spot where Maule's log hut had once stood. Villagers throughout New England were very superstitious at that time, and gossiped that the mansion was built on top of a restless grave, which would give the ghost of Matthew Maule the right to haunt all the rooms in the mansion.

When the gossip reached Colonel Pyncheon's ears, he ridiculed Maule's prediction. "Nobody can threaten me with evil spirits!" he cried.

Even when the clear, fresh water in the spring on the property turned slimy and foul and the townspeople took it as a curse and warned the colonel, he ignored them and continued construction on Pyncheon House.

The finest carpenter in town was hired to head the construction job, even though Thomas Maule was the son of Matthew Maule. His work was so fine that The House of the Seven Gables would stand for two hundred years and even beyond.

When the mansion was completed, Colonel Pyncheon arranged a huge housewarming party. When the festive day arrived it seemed odd, that the colonel—who was known as a courteous gentleman—was not in the front hall to greet his guests.

He Stomped to the Study Door.

Even the governor was stopped by the butler at the front door. "My master is in his study, sir," said the servant, "he left orders not to be disturbed."

"Ridiculous!" cried the governor, "I shall take charge of the situation myself." And he stomped to the study door and knocked loudly.

There was no reply.

He knocked again. Still no reply. His face grew red with anger as he drew out his sword and banged the door with its heavy handle.

The guests watched in bewilderment. "That was loud enough to wake the dead," whispered one woman. But the silence continued behind the study door.

"That's very strange!" the governor exclaimed. "Well, since our host chooses to ignore politeness and courtesy, I shall ignore it too." And he flung open the door.

The crowd pressed toward the door, pushing the governor inside. The room appeared as a normal study should, with bookshelves, a handsome desk, and a large map of the Eastern

Lands and a portrait of Colonel Pyncheon on the wall. Beneath the portrait sat the colonel himself with a pen in his hand. He seemed to be gazing at the crowd frowning at them for having intruded on his privacy.

Suddenly, a young boy broke through the crowd and ran toward the colonel. "Grandfather! Grandfather!" he called. The boy stopped and shrieked in terror.

The crowd drew near and saw blood on the colonel's collar. The governor approached, but there was nothing he or anyone else could do. Colonel Pyncheon was dead.

Then, from among the guests came a voice that to some ears sounded like old Matthew Maule, the legendary wizard. It boomed out, "God hath given him blood to drink!"

Many rumors spread throughout the town for days afterward; weeks, months, and even years after the colonel's death, people suspected he was murdered.

"There were finger marks on the colonel's throat."

Beneath the Portrait Sat the Colonel.

"A bloody handprint was on his shirt."

"The governor saw a skeleton's hand but it vanished when he came close."

"A window in the study was open and a man was seen climbing over the garden fence."

In spite of all these rumors, the town's doctors and a coroner's jury declared that the colonel's death was caused by a stroke.

Colonel Pyncheon left his estate to his son, along with orders that the map and his portrait were to remain in the study forever. But the claim surrounding that map created problems for the family. Just before his death, the colonel was in the midst of settling his claim to this huge territory. It is land that is now the entire state of Maine.

After his death, the documents that could prove his claim were never found.

During the next hundred years, this land was granted to other powerful people and to settlers as well. So all the later Pyncheons could do was hope to gain some of what they believed to be theirs, fooling themselves into believing that their family was still very important and powerful.

The next notable event in the family occurred 150 years after Colonel Pyncheon's death. It was the violent murder of a wealthy old bachelor, Jaffrey Pyncheon. This gentleman, who had never married, often spent his time going through old family records. When he read about the colonel and Matthew Maule, he decided that the wizard had been cheated out of his home and land. Jaffrey wanted to return everything to Maule's descendants.

Some people believed the Pyncheons were afraid of losing their mansion and lands, and that a nephew who was living with the old bachelor had murdered him. The nephew, Clifford Pyncheon, was tried and convicted of the crime. But because the evidence was not completely convincing, the young man was sentenced to life in prison rather than death.

The inheritance passed on to another

He Became a Judge.

nephew, who was also named Jaffrey Pyncheon. This young man had been dishonest and wicked in his youth, but in his later years he had become a respected gentleman with a large mansion outside of town. He studied law and eventually became a judge.

As for Clifford Pyncheon's fate, stories spread after he had served thirty years in prison that he was now to be set free.

By this time, the Pyncheon family was almost dying out. The remaining ones were Judge Jaffrey Pyncheon, and his son, who was traveling in Europe, the prisoner Clifford Pyncheon, and his sister Hepzibah, an old woman who had never married and who had the right to live in The House of the Seven Gables according to the old bachelor's will. And there was the youngest Pyncheon, Miss Phoebe, a country girl of seventeen whose late father was one of Judge Jaffrey Pyncheon's cousins.

As for the descendants of Matthew Maule—they were quiet, honest, poor people who kept to themselves. They worked hard on the wharves or went to sea or were carpenters. But no matter how many years passed or how many generations lived, the superstitious people of this quiet New England town still regarded all Maules with terror; they believed the Maules had mysterious powers, and could even control people's dreams.

At the time this story begins, Pyncheon Street was no longer a fashionable section of town, and Pyncheon House, as The House of the Seven Gables was also called, seemed to be keeping its own secrets. The hundred-year-old Pyncheon Elm was now gigantic as it swept over the house's roof.

One feature of the house had changed since the original construction. A Pyncheon of a hundred years earlier was in need of money. Rather than go out to work, which was undignified for a Pyncheon, he cut a door through the front gable to operate a shop from the house. Even opening a shop at home was regarded as

The Pyncheon Elm Was Gigantic.

a shameful thing for a Pyncheon to have to do, so when this Pyncheon died, his heirs locked and bolted the door.

But for years after his death, townspeople walking by claimed to have looked through the window this man had cut into the door, and seen his ghost! And the ghost was wearing the man's usual shopkeeper's apron over a fancy shirt with lace cuffs.

So, with the histories of the Pyncheons and the Maules, we travel to the 1850s, to begin our story of *The House of the Seven Gables*.

CHAPTER 2

Opening a Penny-Shop

The sun was not up yet when Miss Hepzibah Pyncheon got out of bed. Heaving deep sighs and groans, she knelt for her morning prayers. She desperately needed God's help to see her through this day.

For more than twenty-five years, Hepzibah had lived alone in The House of the Seven Gables. She had no friends, and it was only for the past three months that the house had another living soul under its roof. This was a respectable young man, who made daguerreotypes, photographs made in those days by

23

She Paraded Herself Back and Forth.

transferring an image onto a metal plate and developing it by exposing it to the sun. The photographer, a Mr. Holgrave, had rented rooms in the gable adjoining Hepzibah's, but it was locked off from her gable.

Once Hepzibah was dressed, she paraded back and forth in front of the mirror.

The reflection showed a simple woman in her sixties wearing a black dress turned rusty from age. Her head was wrapped in a turban and her face looked back at her with a scowl that never went away. The scowl was not caused by anger; rather, it was due to poor eye-sight. But to anyone who might see her, Hepzibah appeared to be an angry old maid.

Just before leaving her bedroom, Hepzibah inserted a small key into a secret drawer in her desk. She took out a miniature portrait, and gazed at it lovingly. It was of a handsome young man in an old-fashioned silk robe.

Was it a man she loved when she was young? No, Miss Hepzibah Pyncheon had never been in love, but the portrait, as always, brought tears to her eyes.

With a final look in the mirror, she wiped away the tears and went along the darkened hallway and down the stairs.

She walked slowly; being nearsighted, she wanted to avoid bumping into the old, worn furniture in the room she entered. It was a room that we are familiar with, that had not changed since it was the study where old Colonel Pyncheon had died two hundred years before.

It still had his armchair, bookcases and tables. And on the wall, still hanging, was the large map of the Eastern Lands that was the center of the dispute between the Pyncheons and Maules long ago.

Hepzibah stared at the portrait of the old colonel himself, standing with a Bible in one hand and his sword in the other. The scowl on her face seemed to show anger but it was this kind, good-natured lady's nearsightedness that caused her to squint, which came across as an angry scowl.

The Portrait Brought Tears to Her Eyes.

Miss Hepzibah turned to go into the shop that had been almost untouched since the death of the Pyncheon shopkeeper a hundred years earlier.

For the past several weeks, Hepzibah had busied herself brushing away cobwebs and washing the floor, shelves, and counters. The shop was now stocked with barrels of flour, apples and cornmeal, plus boxes of soap, candles, sugar, beans and peas. There were candies and animal-shaped gingerbread cookies.

This was the scene that greeted Hepzibah as she opened the hallway door and entered the shop.

As she began rearranging some toys and cookies in the window, Hepzibah realized that she was no longer the aristocratic lady of the Pyncheon family waiting for wealth from owning the Eastern Lands. She was now a working woman who was forced to open a penny-shop in her old age to keep from starving. Hepzibah dreaded having people see her reduced to working as a common shopkeeper after the generations of important, aristocratic, wealthy Pyncheons who came before her.

But as the sun began pouring into the shop through the branches of the Pyncheon Elm, Hepzibah knew that the moment had arrived when she had to face the world. Reluctantly she took down the bar across the shop's door. But suddenly she ran back into the study and threw herself into the colonel's old armchair.

"I cannot do it!" she sobbed into her hands. "I can-"

But the little bell on top of the shop's door interrupted her weeping and announced that a customer had entered the shop.

Hepzibah trembled as she gripped the arms of the chair and stood up. Her pale face suddenly turned wild as she panicked. I must smile, she told herself, but I'd much rather be going anywhere but into that shop!

"Can I Be of Help?"

CHAPTER 3

The First Customers

The customer Hepzibah found inside the shop was the pleasant-looking young man who rented rooms in the mansion—the young photographer. He was about twenty-two years old.

"Good morning, Miss Hepzibah," said Mr. Holgrave with a smile. "I'm off to my studio to do some daguerreotypes, but I just wanted to stop by to wish you good luck and to tell you how glad I am to see that you were brave enough to open the shop. Can I be of any help to you?"

After Holgrave left, Hepzibah's spirits

seemed to brighten from his encouragement.

She stayed in the shop watching people pass by. Some passed without even a look, while others stopped briefly to glance into her shop window.

Two workmen approached. One pointed to the window and exclaimed, "Well, who would have thought that Old Maid Pyncheon would open a penny-shop!"

"Do you think she'll succeed?" said the other.

"Succeed? Ha! With that face, she'd frighten any customer away. That scowl of hers proves she's just a mean-tempered old woman. Besides, my own wife tried to open a penny-shop and it lasted only three months. I lost every bit of money I put into it."

Hepzibah overheard this conversation and it hurt her deeply. "How can these men enjoy humiliating me? If that man's hard-working wife failed in her shop, how could I expect to succeed? I'm certain not one foot will enter my shop."

It Hurt Her Deeply.

As Hepzibah turned away, the shop bell jingled again and the door was flung open. The sad, gentle lady jumped and her heart began to pound. She turned to see a sturdy young boy of about twelve or thirteen in shabby but clean clothes. He was carrying a book and a small writing slate under his arm. Hepzibah recognized him from the neighborhood.

"Well," said Hepzibah, "why have you stopped here on your way to school, Ned Higgins?"

"I'd like that gingerbread cookie in the window," said Ned as he held out his penny to pay for it.

Hepzibah took the cookie from the window and handed it to the boy. "You are welcome to the cookie, Ned. No need for money." Hepzibah could not bear to be mean and take the boy's money to pay for a bit of stale gingerbread.

Ned's eyes widened as he exclaimed, "No one in any penny-shop has ever given me a gingerbread cookie for free!" And he hurried out the door, quickly stuffing the cookie into his mouth before the shopkeeper could change her mind.

Hepzibah was just replacing the ginger-bread man in the window when the bell jingled again. It was Ned Higgins again, this time with a face covered with crumbs.

"What is it now, child?" Hepzibah asked.

"I want the other gingerbread man," said the boy, pointing to the window.

Hepzibah realized that the boy would keep coming back if she continued giving him free cookies, so she asked, "Where is your penny?"

Ned had it ready even though he had a look of disappointment on his face.

Once Ned had gone, Hepzibah put his penny into the cashbox. "Now I am no longer a lady," she said with a sigh. "I'm only Hepzibah Pyncheon, a sad old maid who is nothing but a lowly shopkeeper."

After a while, Hepzibah's anxiety and sad-ness began to disappear. She looked again at the round copper penny in the cashbox and thought to herself, This little coin will become

Hepzibah Felt Almost Proud!

my good-luck charm. It proves to me that my shop will take away the loneliness of my old life, and that in my new life I can help myself.

One haggard woman—the wife of a drunken husband and the mother of nine children—came in for some flour. Kindly Miss Hepzibah gave her more flour than she had asked for, then refused to take any money from the tired-looking overworked young woman.

Still, there were other customers who criticized Hepzibah and shouted at her rudely; who treated the gentle old lady as if they were superior to her.

And when she saw some of the aristocratic ladies pass by, Hepzibah remembered Mr. Holgrave's words about these idle rich ladies having no purpose in life. They are just as I was once, expecting everyone to serve them! She told herself.

Hepzibah felt almost proud of herself!

CHAPTER 4

A Day Behind the Counter

Hepzibah went up to her bedroom and took out the miniature from her secret drawer. She gazed at it lovingly as she said, "How gentle you were, so much like our loving mother. That was why Cousin Jaffrey hated you. You were never like the evil Pyncheons!"

The tinkling of the shop bell interrupted Hepzibah's memories. She quickly put the portrait away and hurried downstairs.

"Good afternoon, Uncle Venner," Hepzibah said to the ancient-looking, wrinkled man who had just entered the shop.

"Good Afternoon, Uncle Venner."

Uncle Venner wasn't really anybody's uncle; he was the neighborhood handyman. Many people considered him slow-witted. since he was a young man, but Hepzibah appreciated his good sense and wisdom.

Although his clothes were castoffs from people in town, Uncle Venner wore them proudly even though his body was bent over.

"So, Miss Hepzibah," he greeted her, "you have really opened your business. Everyone should work until they're too old or too sick. I figure in about two or three years, I'll have to stop working and retire to my farm."

"Thank you, Uncle Venner," Hepzibah said, smiling. She knew that the old man's "farm" was really the poorhouse. "It seems I'm just beginning to work at an age when most people are giving it up and retiring."

"Never say that, Miss Hepzibah, for you are still a young woman. By the way, I passed the judge on the street a while ago. He bowed and smiled at me, an unusual thing for a

Pyncheon gentleman to do. But, if I may ask, Miss Hepzibah, why doesn't Judge Pyncheon, with all his money tell you to close the shop and help you out?"

"I really don't wish to talk about this, please, Uncle Venner. I have chosen to earn my way. If I cannot, I suppose I'll retire to your farm too."

Uncle Venner went on to give her some business advice.

"Don't give any credit. Don't take any paper money, only copper or silver coins. Watch the change you give. In your free time, knit children's socks and mittens. And prepare your own yeast and ginger beer."

With that, Uncle Venner bent forward and whispered, "When do you expect him home?"

Hepzibah turned pale. "Who do you mean?"

"I guess you don't want to talk about it, but the word is out all over town that Clifford is on his way here. And remember, Hepzibah, I knew him when he was a baby, before he could even walk by himself."

41

A Pretty Young Girl Jumped Down.

Sensing that Hepzibah wanted to be alone now, Uncle Venner left. The old woman busied herself as customers came into the shop, although her mind wasn't on her work. She gave wrong change, brought out pins for needles and needles for pins, made errors weighing her products, and gave Ned a wooden dragon when he asked for a gingerbread elephant.

By the end of the day, Hepzibah had earned six cents. She was happy when she finally put the metal bar across the door and was about to turn to go into the house when she spotted a carriage pulling up, stopping under the Pyncheon Elm.

Hepzibah caught her breath. "Can that be Clifford now?" she gasped.

But it was a pretty young girl with curly brown hair and a face full of freckles who jumped down from the carriage. The driver carried her trunk along the path to the front door of The House of the Seven Gables and rapped on it with the old iron knocker.

Hepzibah hurried to the door and tried to focus her nearsighted eyes through the window on the cheerful young face waiting outside. She must be at the wrong house, Hepzibah thought. No, wait. Can it be Phoebe, Phoebe Pyncheon? She does resemble her late father. But what can she want here? It certainly isn't proper for a country cousin to come for a visit without notice. Well, I'll surely let her stay overnight, but tomorrow I'll have to send her back to her mother.

Actually, people in New England at that time did visit relatives without an invitation and without warning. But because Phoebe knew of Hepzibah's isolated life, she had made certain to send a letter. But the letter stayed in the postman's pocket for many days since he had no other mail to deliver to Pyncheon Street.

As she prepared to unlock the front door, Hepzibah confirmed the decision she had made minutes ago. "She can stay only one night," she whispered. "If Clifford were to find her or anyone else here, it might upset him."

"She Can Only Stay One Night."

CHAPTER 5

Phoebe Pyncheon Arrives

"I'm only here for a visit, Cousin Hepzibah. My mother has remarried and I find life at home most unhappy," Phoebe explained.

"We will talk in the morning, Cousin Phoebe," said Hepzibah as she showed the young girl to a room facing east, overlooking the garden.

So, it was the morning sun that greeted Phoebe when she awoke. A look out the window revealed a garden with a beautiful bush of white roses directly below her.

Phoebe dressed quietly and hurried down

46

the creaking wooden staircase. She gathered some of the roses and brought them up to her room.

The young girl set about rearranging the dark and dreary room, which had not been occupied for many years. Phoebe hoped to make it more pleasant and cozy. With the curtains open and the roses giving off their sweet scent, the room was becoming bright and cheerful.

As Phoebe went down to the garden for more flowers, she met Hepzibah.

"Please, Cousin Phoebe, come into my room for a few minutes," said Hepzibah. "I'd like to talk to you."

Phoebe entered her cousin's room. She looked around at the dusty writing desk and another piece of furniture that looked like a coffin to her.

"You are admiring the family harpsichord," said the old woman. "It hasn't been played since Miss Alice Pyncheon played it years and years ago. It is her room you are sleeping in."

When both women were seated, Hepzibah explained, "Cousin Phoebe, I understand that

"I Only Want to Visit."

your life has been somewhat uncomfortable at home since your mother remarried, and I understand that you feel you need to live elsewhere. But there really isn't any way I can let you live here with me."

"Please, dear Cousin Hepzibah," said Phoebe, "I only want to visit for a week or two, unless we both decide we like living together. And I do think we might."

"Dear girl, this house is a cold, gloomy place for a young girl, and I am a gloomy, lonely old woman. Besides, I do not have the money to support you."

"I do not wish you to do that," said Phoebe. "I want to earn my keep. Even though my name is Pyncheon, I have been raised in the country, far away from the wealthy Pyncheons. I could take care of the garden for you and—"

Hepzibah rose to her feet and stated firmly, "Child, the decision as to who lives in The House of the Seven Gables is not mine to make. The master of this house is not here now, but he is coming soon."

"Its master?" asked Phoebe, puzzled. "Do you mean Judge Pyncheon?"

"Judge Pyncheon!" cried Hepzibah furiously. "No! That man will not be allowed inside this door as long as I am alive. I will show you who the true master of this house is." Hepzibah went to her secret drawer and showed Phoebe the miniature portrait she kept there.

"How do you like him?" asked Hepzibah.

"He is very handsome, a sweet, kindly face. He seems to have a child's expression. Who is he, Cousin Hepzibah?"

"You never heard of Clifford Pyncheon?"

"No, I thought you and Cousin Jaffrey were the only Pyncheons left. I seem to remember my father once mentioning a cousin Clifford. But hasn't he been dead for many years?"

"Perhaps he has been," said Hepzibah with a sad laugh. "But in a house like this, dead people often come back to life. You have courage, dear Phoebe. If after all that I have said, you still want to stay and live here, you are

"You Never Heard of Clifford?"

welcome." Hepzibah bent to kiss Phoebe's cheek.

Phoebe began making breakfast for them. The young girl sang happily while the old woman clumsily set the table.

"You must have learned from your mother's side of the family," Hepzibah said, "for no Pyncheon lady was ever so ambitious."

"Thank you, Cousin Hepzibah. I do not consider myself a fancy lady. I not only cook, but I even worked as a teacher in our village. I would probably still be teaching today if things at home had not changed."

As the two were finishing, they heard the jingle of the shop bell. Hepzibah put down her teacup, a look of despair on her face. For a few minutes she had felt like a Pyncheon lady again, with Phoebe preparing her breakfast and the two of them drinking their tea from the delicate family teacups.

"Oh, how I hate that bell! I hate the thought of facing customers again today!" Hepzibah moaned as she rose from her place at the head of the table.

"Do not bother, dear cousin," Phoebe said brightly, jumping up. "I shall be the shopkeeper today!"

"You, child?" Hepzibah chided gently. "What can a little country girl know about running a shop?"

"I've done all the shopping for our family for years," Phoebe answered, "and I have had a table at many fairs where I sold more goods than anyone else. I seem to have a knack for selling. You'll see, Cousin Hepzibah."

Once Phoebe entered the shop, Hepzibah peeped through the door to watch. An old woman who spun yarn came in to trade her yarn for some goods. The old woman was sly and crafty, but Phoebe used honesty and wisdom to bargain well.

"Nicely done, child!" said Hepzibah admiringly as Phoebe returned to the kitchen, laughing.

Phoebe dealt with all the customers for the rest of the day. When the shop wasn't busy, the two spent their time discussing how to increase business.

Ned Made Three Visits.

Once the neighborhood people met Phoebe, they returned more and more often, starting that very day. The most frequent of all Phoebe's customers was Ned Higgins, who on that particular day made three visits to the shop and bought two gingerbread camels and one gingerbread train.

Uncle Venner stopped in several times and praised Phoebe as one of God's angels.

Once Phoebe had closed the shop for the day, Hepzibah put on a pair of gloves to count the mountains of coins, while Phoebe added up the day's sales on a slate.

"We must prepare new merchandise," Phoebe said. "All the gingerbread animals and toys are gone. We need more raisins and whistles and trumpets, too. And dozens of boys have asked for molasses candy."

After their business plans were made, Hepzibah asked Phoebe, "Would you like to see the entire house now, dear cousin?"

"Oh, yes, thank you!" Phoebe answered with all her young enthusiasm.

Hepzibah went from room to room, telling Phoebe the family stories about each one.

"Here, Phoebe, you see the dents in the study door? They were made by the governor's sword handle just before he opened the door and found old Colonel Pyncheon dead at his desk."

Hepzibah continued. "Climb up on this chair, child, and look at this ancient map. This is Pyncheon land to the east. There's a valuable silver mine on this land which will belong to the family when the government recognizes the Pyncheon claim."

Hepzibah helped Phoebe down from the chair. "There is also a legend of an immense treasure of English gold hidden somewhere in The House of the Seven Gables or in the garden. And if you find it, dear Phoebe, we will close the shop for good!"

The two women continued their tour of the house. When they reached Phoebe's room, Hepzibah told her young cousin its story.

"This room belonged to Alice Pyncheon a hundred years ago. She was a very beautiful and

They Went from Room to Room.

talented young woman who played the most wonderful music on the harpsichord. She died very young and very mysteriously. It is said that even now she haunts The House of the Seven Gables by playing on her harpsichord—right before any Pyncheon dies."

"So for the past hundred years, Alice's harpsichord has announced all the Pyncheon deaths?" Phoebe asked.

"Yes, and because of that legend, I wasn't allowed to play on it. Even though my father let me take lessons, I had to play on my teacher's harpsichord."

They left Phoebe's room and went downstairs and continued along the hallway. As they passed a heavy wooden door with a lock on it, Hepzibah explained, "This door leads to the gable where Mr. Holgrave, a photographer, lives. He has been renting rooms from me for about three months. He seemed to be a pleasant enough young man when I rented the rooms to him."

"And have you now changed your opinion of him?" Phoebe asked curious.

"I'm not certain. I read a story in the newspaper about his making wild speeches and having friends who did not seem very respectable types. I personally believe he has some strange powers and exerts a great influence over these friends. It's almost as if he hypnotizes them into doing his bidding."

"But, Cousin Hepzibah, if you consider the young man so dangerous, why do you let him stay here?"

"I have thought about that often, but he is a quiet, polite person and has a way of making me fond of him. And an old woman as lonely as I am is grateful for any acquaintance."

Phoebe leaned forward and grasped her cousin's hand. "You won't be lonely anymore, dear Hepzibah. I promise."

Hepzibah's eyes filled with tears.

Phoebe Went into the Garden.

CHAPTER 6

Maule's Well

That same afternoon after the shop had closed, Phoebe went out into the garden. Three of the house's seven gables faced the garden, where the black soil had been made rich and fertile by decayed leaves, flowers and seeds that had been piling up over the years.

Having grown up in the country, Phoebe knew that the fruit trees had been pruned quite recently and that the vegetable and flower beds had been carefully weeded.

"Who can be caring for these tomatoes and cucumbers and string beans and squashes?" she wondered aloud. "It surely isn't

Cousin Hepzibah, for she wouldn't spend any time to weed and hoe a garden."

Phoebe saw a fountain surrounded by moss-covered rocks. Walking closer to admire it, Phoebe saw through the water that the bottom of the fountain held different-colored pebbles. These pebbles seemed to create strange shapes as the water gushed up and swirled around.

After Phoebe had spent several minutes watching, she walked toward the hen coop in the far corner of the garden.

The coop was the home of a rooster named Chanticleer, his two hens and one lone chick. This family's ancestors had been with the Pyncheon family since The House of the Seven Gables was built. Over years of neglect and poor feeding, they had gone from the size of turkeys in the colonel's time to the size of pigeons in Hepzibah's.

To the little family she said, "I shall get you some bread and cold potatoes from the kitchen."

The Coop Was Their Home.

When Phoebe returned, she made a strange sound which the fowl seemed to recognize. The little chick even crept through the wire of the coop and ran to her. It fluttered up to her shoulder as Chanticleer and the hens began clucking in the coop.

From behind Phoebe came a man's voice. "That little chicken pays you a compliment."

Phoebe spun around and saw a young man with a hoe in his hand coming out of another gable.

The young man added with a smile, "That chicken treats you like an old friend. Even the family in the coop seems to like you, too. You are lucky to have made friends so soon. They have known me much longer and even though I bring them food they don't consider me a friend. Perhaps it is because they know you are a Pyncheon."

Phoebe couldn't help but smile. She immediately realized that this man was the photographer Hepzibah had told her about.

"The secret is that I have learned how to

talk with hens and chickens. But you are correct. I am a Pyncheon, Phoebe Pyncheon."

"And I am Holgrave," he said. "I live in that gable. In my free time I enjoy working here in the garden, digging and hoeing and weeding."

"And what is your occupation in your work time, Mr. Holgrave?" Phoebe asked.

"I work with sunshine. I make pictures, especially portraits, using sunshine on metal plates. Would you care to see a sample of my daguerreotypes?" he asked.

"Any I have ever seen appear to be disagreeable, unfriendly people," Phoebe replied.

"Perhaps the sunshine that's used to make a picture brings out the evil in a person. People smile for the portrait and appear nice and friendly, but deep inside, they may not be. An artist paints what he sees on a person's face, but the sunshine reveals the secret truth of a person's character."

Holgrave took a small leather case out of his pocket and opened it up. "See, the person here is seen by people he meets each day as kind,

"I Know That Face."

friendly and generous—but the daguerreotype shows him as he really is, an evil man!"

Phoebe glanced at the daguerreotype for a moment. "I know that face. I see it every day on the wall. It is my ancestor, Colonel Pyncheon. You have found a way to copy his portrait and take away his gray beard. You dressed him in a modern suit instead of the Puritan clothes in the portrait. And you have put a gold-tipped walking stick in his hand instead of a sword."

Mr. Holgrave laughed. "You would have seen other differences if you had looked a little longer. This is a modern face, not the old colonel's. The sunshine that exposes the metal plates of photographs shows he is a sly, hard, cold and evil man. And it is sad because he is a well-known public official whom you will probably meet one day very soon."

"Miss Hepzibah has another portrait, a miniature she treasures. If the person in that picture exists, the sun would never make that sweet, gentle face look stern and hard," Phoebe said.

"Tell me, do you think the person in that picture could have committed a crime?" Holgrave asked.

"That's nonsense!" Phoebe snapped, losing patience. "You have never seen that picture. How can you say he has committed a crime?"

"Because that person has been tried and found guilty of murder by a judge and jury! But please, let us talk of pleasant things. It would give me great pleasure to turn over the care of Miss Hepzibah's flowers to you, while I provide the good lady with vegetables."

Phoebe agreed and quietly began to weed the flower bed. But her thoughts were on the young man hoeing the rows of vegetables. He is a puzzle to me, she thought. I don't like him, but I don't dislike him either. He is very polite, but I almost get the feeling that he has a power over me. Phoebe and Holgrave worked in the garden until darkness crept in. As Holgrave turned to enter his gable door, he called to

Phoebe Began to Weed the Flower Bed.

Phoebe, "If you would like to visit my studio on Center Street, I would be happy to do a portrait of you. And by the way," he added, pointing to the fountain Phoebe had seen earlier, "be careful not to drink that water and don't wash your face in it, either. That's Maule's Well!"

"Maule's Well?" Phoebe asked. "Is that what it's called? I hadn't thought of drinking from it—but why not?"

"Because the water in Maule's Well is bewitched!" he called back over his shoulder as he disappeared inside his door.

Phoebe chuckled at Holgrave's words, then went back inside Hepzibah's gable. She found her cousin sitting in the study in complete darkness.

"Shall I light a lamp, Cousin Hepzibah?" she asked.

"If you wish so, child, but put it far away from me. Put it in the hallway. The lamplight hurts my eyes."

Then Phoebe heard the murmur of an unknown voice. Did I imagine someone other than Cousin Hepzibah speaking in the study? she wondered.

Phoebe set the lamp on a hall table and entered the study, which was just as dark as before. "Did you call to me a moment ago, Cousin?" she asked Hepzibah.

"No, child," answered the old woman, with a tremble in her voice.

Phoebe sat down silently, but in a moment she soon sensed that someone else was breathing in a dark corner of the room. "Cousin Hepzibah," she whispered hesitantly, "is there someone in the room with us?"

"Child, you have been up since early morning and you have been busy all day," said Hepzibah. "Go to bed now. I need to sit in the study for a while. It has been my habit since before you were born."

Hepzibah got up from her chair and took Phoebe in her arms. She kissed her young cousin and hugged her with more love than Phoebe had ever received before in her young life.

"Good night, Cousin Hepzibah," Phoebe

Were There Strange Things Happening?

said, greatly affected by Hepzibah's display of love. "If you are beginning to love me, I am so very glad!"

Although Phoebe went up to her room, she didn't fall asleep immediately. As she lay awake, she heard heavy footsteps climbing the stairs. Along with those footsteps, she heard Hepzibah whispering and a strange low murmuring answering her cousin. It was the same murmuring she had heard when she was in the kitchen lighting the lamp.

Were there strange things happening at The House of the Seven Gables?

CHAPTER 7

The Return of Clifford Pyncheon

When Phoebe awoke the next morning, she heard Hepzibah in the kitchen. Hurrying down, Phoebe found her cousin standing by a window holding a cookbook at the tip of her nose, trying to read it.

"I want to make something special for breakfast," Hepzibah said. "Can you see if one of the hens has laid an egg?"

Phoebe ran out to check, but returned empty-handed. "I'm sorry, Cousin. But wait! I just heard the fish peddler in the street. He's here with fish to sell."

"Wonderful!" Hepzibah said. She ran into

"I Want to Make Something Special."

the shop and knocked to get the peddler's attention.

Hepzibah selected a fine mackerel. Phoebe began preparing it for breakfast.

Hepzibah nervously set the table for three in the dining room, with a fine damask cloth, her best china cups and plates, and the engraved Pyncheon silver. Phoebe filled a pitcher with beautiful red roses from the garden and got warm thanks from Hepzibah.

"He loves beautiful things," she said.

Once the table and the food were ready, Hepzibah stepped back to admire it. Only the old colonel's surly face, scowling down from his portrait, seemed as if he were showing his annoyance at their breakfast celebration.

Phoebe couldn't help wonder whom the third place-setting at the table was for.

Hepzibah took Phoebe's hand in hers. "Please forgive my nervousness and my irritability this morning. My heart is full of love for you, and I promise I will never do anything to hurt you."

"Dear Cousin Hepzibah, you haven't done anything to hurt me. But can you tell me what has happened?" Phoebe pleaded. "Why are you upset one moment and overjoyed the next?"

"He's coming!" Hepzibah whispered. "Let him see you first. You are young and pretty and always smiling. Clifford always liked bright and smiling faces. My face is old and covered with tears, and Clifford hates tears. I must open the curtains and let the sunshine in. He hates gloomy places. Poor Clifford!"

Just then, Phoebe heard footsteps coming slowly and heavily down the stairs.

Hepzibah began to tremble.

"Cousin Hepzibah," said Phoebe, "you are frightening me."

"Hush!" Hepzibah whispered. "Smile and be cheerful no matter what happens."

She threw the door open and gently led a strange-looking old man into the room.

Phoebe looked at the stranger. His nearly white hair was long, down to his shoulders and hanging over his forehead. His face had a child-

Clifford Pyncheon Was Home.

like expression with eyes that started out shining, then quickly turned to a dull, vacant stare.

The old man looked around the room slowly. When he spotted Phoebe, he made an attempt to bow gracefully to her.

Hepzibah continued to hold the old man's hand and in a soft voice that one would use to a baby, she said, "Clifford, this is Cousin Phoebe. She has come to stay with us a while."

"Phoebe? Phoebe Pyncheon? Phoebe?" the old man repeated slowly and dully. "Ah, I forgot. No matter, she is very welcome."

Hepzibah led her brother to his place at the head of the table. Once he was seated, he started looking around as if to be sure he knew where he was.

Phoebe sat staring at Clifford until she suddenly realized where she had seen him. He is the handsome young man in Hepzibah's miniature picture, she said to herself. His worn face and body show much suffering since the portrait was done.

Hepzibah poured a cup of coffee for Clifford and set it before him. As his eyes met hers, he seemed bewildered, even troubled.

"Is this you, Hepzibah?" he murmured sadly, more to himself than to his sister. "You have changed so much. Are you angry with me that you are frowning?"

Poor Hepzibah! That frown and scowl were only the result of her poor eyesight, but she placed her hand tenderly on Clifford's and replied, "Angry? There is no anger here, Clifford. There is only love here."

Clifford sat back. He studied the room around him. "How pleasant! How delightful!" he whispered. Then his face darkened.

Phoebe took a rose from the vase and offered it to him to distract him. "Look at the new kind of rose I found this morning, Cousin Clifford. It is perfect in its red color and its scent is unforgettable."

"Let me hold it!" cried Clifford, seizing the flower. "I remember how I used to prize these flowers so very long ago... or was it yesterday?

"There Is Only Love Here."

It makes me feel young again!"

But Clifford's joy did not last long, for as he was reaching out to take Phoebe's hand in his to thank her, his eyes came to rest on the portrait of Colonel Pyncheon.

Turning to Hepzibah, he cried, "Why do you keep that hateful picture of that evil man on the wall? Take it down at once!"

"Dear Clifford," said Hepzibah sadly, "you know that I cannot. The old colonel's will stated that his portrait must stay on the wall as long as The House of the Seven Gables stands."

"Then cover it with a large cloth!" Clifford ordered. "And do it this very day!"

This outburst exerted so much effort on his frail old body that Clifford's eyes began to close. Within minutes, he was sound asleep in his chair.

Moments later, the ringing of the shop's bell woke him with a sudden start. "Good Heavens, Hepzibah!" he cried out. "What is that terrible noise disturbing our house? Why do you allow it?"

Phoebe hurried into the shop, leaving Hepzibah to calm her brother.

The old woman took Clifford's hand in hers and explained patiently. "I wish I could keep that sound from disturbing you. It disturbs me too. But it is our shop's bell."

"Shop's bell?" repeated Clifford, with a puzzled look.

"Yes, dear Clifford, you must know the truth," Hepzibah explained. "We are now very poor. I had two choices in order to keep us alive. I could accept help from Cousin Jaffrey, which neither you nor I would ever do. Or I could earn money with my own hands by opening up the old penny-shop here in the gable again. Please don't be ashamed of me for doing it, dear brother."

"Ashamed! No," Clifford said sadly. "I have brought enough shame to our family. There is nothing more that can hurt me." And with a great sigh of sadness, and tears rolling down his wrinkled cheeks, Clifford sank into

She Closed the Curtains.

the softness of his armchair. He was soon in a deep sleep.

Hepzibah studied her brother's sleeping face, and her heart broke at seeing how he had aged and wasted away in prison. She closed the curtains to darken the room and left Clifford to his peaceful sleep.

CHAPTER 8

Judge Jaffrey Pyncheon

The customer waiting to greet Phoebe when she entered the shop was young Ned Higgins. He had spent all of his pennies on gingerbread cookies the day before and was there to buy three eggs for his mother.

Once the sale had been completed, Phoebe handed the boy a gingerbread whale, which was soon swallowed as quickly as the whale had swallowed Jonah in the Bible story.

With his mouth full of his treat, Ned said, "Mother wants to know how Miss Pyncheon's brother is, now that he's home from prison."

"From prison!" Phoebe gasped. "I had no

The Customer Waiting Was Ned.

idea that is where Clifford has been."

As Ned hurried down the shop's steps, he passed a well-dressed elderly gentleman in a fine black suit walking up the steps. The smile on his face seemed to be frozen there without any real feeling behind it. But this was typical of Judge Jaffrey Pyncheon.

Many people were fooled into thinking this smile was genuine and showed the judge to be a good, kind man. But a few people knew better.

The judge entered the shop and was surprised to see young Phoebe behind the counter instead of his old maid cousin. "I didn't know that Miss Hepzibah Pyncheon had opened her shop with such success that she needed an assistant already," he said.

"I am her assistant," said Phoebe proudly. "But I am not a worker here. I am Miss Hepzibah Pyncheon's cousin, here visiting her from my home in the country."

"Aha!" exclaimed the judge, bowing and smiling at Phoebe. "Then, my dear, we must get to know each other, for I am your cousin too. You must be Phoebe Pyncheon, the only child of my dear cousin Arthur. I am your cousin, Judge Jaffrey Pyncheon."

Phoebe curtsied to him and the judge leaned over the counter to give her an affectionate kiss. Unfortunately, for whatever instinct made her do it, Phoebe drew back, leaving the judge's extended lips kissing the empty air.

Phoebe lowered her eyes and blushed, but when she raised them, she saw that the judge's wide smile had turned into a cold, hard glare.

Then she suddenly remembered the daguerreotype Mr. Holgrave had shown her in the garden. The man in it—the man with the hard, stern, evil face that the sunshine had revealed—was not the old colonel, as she had thought! It was this man, Judge Jaffrey Pyncheon, her cousin!

"I like that, Cousin Phoebe!" the judge exclaimed. "You are a good girl who knows how to take care of herself. A pretty girl like you must never be too free with her kisses to anyone, not even cousins."

"I Did Not Mean to Be Unkind."

Phoebe tried to laugh as she apologized. "I did not mean to be unkind."

But still, her behavior was not like her usual friendly way and her thoughts went spinning around in her head. I feel as if the evil old colonel had stepped into the shop, she thought, with his long beard trimmed. It's as if he changed into modern clothes and switched his sword for that gold-headed cane he carries. It's almost as if Colonel Pyncheon of two hundred years ago is back as Judge Jaffrey Pyncheon.

Then Phoebe remembered the curse Matthew Maule had placed on the colonel and his descendants. And after her apology, when she heard the judge make a noise in his throat—which was a habit with him because of some condition in his lungs—she gasped in horror!

Judge Pyncheon looked at her strangely. "What is the matter with you, young woman?" he asked harshly.

"Oh, nothing, sir," Phoebe answered, a little annoyed with herself for letting her imagination create such fantasies in her mind. Then she politely suggested, "Perhaps you wish to speak to Miss Hepzibah?"

"In a moment," said the judge, now all smiles again. "You seem a bit nervous, Cousin Phoebe. Are you ill? Perhaps something has happened to disturb you? Has a frightful guest arrived and startled such an innocent young girl as yourself?"

"That is a strange question, sir! There is no frightful guest in the house—only a poor, gentle man who is Miss Hepzibah's brother. You must know he is not quite in his right mind. But he is so quiet and gentle, a mother would trust her baby with him. Surely, Cousin Jaffrey, he would never frighten me!"

"That's because you don't really know him," said Judge Pyncheon. "I have known him for years when Clifford and I were growing up together. I still have great affection for him. You say he is weak-minded, but I hope he has enough sanity and enough good sense to repent for his sins."

"In a Moment," Said the Judge.

"A man like him? Sin? Heavens, no!" cried Phoebe.

"Then you know nothing about his history," the judge told her. "Perhaps it is better that you don't. But if Clifford is inside, I'll just stop in and see him."

"Let me ask Miss Hepzibah first," Phoebe said. "I know that Clifford fell asleep right after breakfast. I'm sure she wouldn't want to disturb him."

But the judge was determined to have his way. As Phoebe moved to the door to call Hepzibah, the judge pushed her aside. "Stay here!" he growled. A menacing frown crossed his face. "I don't need to be announced in this house!"

Then his smile returned. "I am at home here, Phoebe, and you are the stranger. So I'll just go in and... oh, here comes Cousin Hepzibah herself," he added.

The devoted old woman had been sitting in the study watching her brother sleep when she heard the judge's demands. Then, just as a fire-breathing fairytale dragon guards an enchanted sleeper, Hepzibah hurried to the shop to defend her brother.

Her scowl was fiercer now from anger than it had ever been from poor eyesight. It was now a raging scowl directed toward the judge in a way that alarmed him, especially when her arm reached out to push him away.

With a broad, even wider smile quickly pasted on his face, the judge reached out his hand to Hepzibah. "Beloved Cousin, I am so happy for you!" he exclaimed. "Now we all have more to live for than we did yesterday. Now that our dear Clifford is back with us again. I hurried here to offer my help in making Clifford comfortable. I know how he always loved the beautiful things in my home—my pictures, my books, my furnishings. I would be happy to give him anything he wants. And I would like to see him now to tell him so."

"No!" Hepzibah declared firmly. "He cannot have visitors."

"How can you call me a visitor?" cried the

"My Brother Has a Home Here."

judge, appearing to be insulted by the word. Then instead, "You and Clifford can come to my house and enjoy all the luxuries I have. Together, we'll make our Clifford happy."

Hearing this generous offer, Phoebe had an urge to run up to the judge and give him the kiss she had backed away from earlier. But the look she saw on Hepzibah's face kept her from doing it.

"No, again!" Hepzibah repeated stubbornly. "My brother has a home here!"

The judge lifted his eyes upward and spoke as if appealing to God. "May Heaven forgive you, Hepzibah, for keeping your brother in this dismal house when he could have the freedom of a country estate."

"A country estate would not suit Clifford," Hepzibah declared steadfastly.

"Woman!" the judge shouted angrily. "How do you plan to support your brother? With almost no money left, you are both close to ruin! Now get out of my way! I must see Clifford!"

Hepzibah spread her arms and legs and blocked the doorway with her entire body. Then, just as the judge was about to force his way past her, a weak and pleading wail came from inside the study.

"Hepzibah! Hepzibah!" Clifford called out. "Don't let him come in! Have mercy on me!"

The sound of Clifford's voice brought rage to the judge's face. He started to take a quick step toward Hepzibah, then drew back. His scowl was replaced by his usual fake smile.

"You are wrong about me, Hepzibah," he said, pretending sweetness. I understand that Clifford is not ready to see anyone. However, I will watch over him as if he were my own brother."

With a bow to Hepzibah and a fatherly smile to Phoebe, Judge Jaffrey Pyncheon turned on his heels and left the shop.

As soon as the door had closed behind him, Hepzibah turned deathly pale and staggered toward Phoebe. "Oh, Phoebe!" she moaned, letting her head fall onto the young girl's shoulder. "That man has been the horror

Hepzibah Blocked the Doorway.

of my life! Will I ever get up enough courage to tell him how wicked he really is?"

"But how can he be wicked when he made such a kind offer to you and Clifford?" asked Phoebe.

"Our cousin has a heart of iron! The smiles he puts on his face are completely false. He is evil! You will see that one day. Now, please go to Clifford. I'm certain you can amuse him and help him forget what he just heard. I cannot go in to him now—I cannot let him see me so upset. I will look after the shop until I am able to calm myself down," Hepzibah said.

Phoebe went into the study to be with Clifford, but she couldn't stop thinking about the judge. She kept asking herself, "How can a judge, a man so important and dignified and respectable, really be as wicked as Cousin Hepzibah claims?"

And being the simple, innocent country girl she was, the only answer Phoebe could come up with out loud was, "There must have been a family feud that caused some bad feelings between Hepzibah and the judge!"

CHAPTER 9

Clifford and Phoebe

Hepzibah now set about trying everything she could think of to begin helping erase the sadness and dreariness of Clifford's past thirty years in prison. She gave him books that had once been his favorites. She read him poetry he had once loved. But nothing helped. The thing that disturbed Hepzibah the most was Clifford's reaction to how she looked.

While Hepzibah had never been really pretty in her youth, grief had caused her to age. Then, too, her anger against the world for what it had done to her beloved brother—plus her old clothes and her dreadful turban—made it

"You Brighten Clifford's Life as Well."

difficult for Clifford, who loved beauty, to look at her.

The lines in her face, which now made her look as if she was always scowling, increased Clifford's response to Hepzibah's dowdy appearance now.

She turned to Phoebe for help, knowing that the girl could give Clifford someone beautiful to look at and spend time with. "The dreariness of Pyncheon House has vanished for me since you came to visit here," Hepzibah told her young cousin, "and now you have begun to brighten Clifford's life as well."

Clifford began to depend on Phoebe so much that if she were away from him for even a little while, he grew nervous and restless. He would either pace the room anxiously, or sit in his chair with his head in his hands, brooding.

If Phoebe went about some work in the house and sang while she was doing it, Clifford was content, as long as he could hear her sweet voice. But Clifford was the happiest when Phoebe sat on a footstool near him and he could hold her hand.

As he spent more and more time with Phoebe, Clifford seemed to grow younger and on his way to returning to the real world. As for Phoebe herself, she began to know Clifford too well to be afraid of him.

Within a few days of Clifford's arrival, life at The House of the Seven Gables had soon settled in to a routine. In the morning after breakfast, Clifford would fall asleep in his chair and nap peacefully until noon. During these hours, Hepzibah kept watch over him, doing her knitting while Phoebe ran the shop.

In the afternoon, Hepzibah took her knitting and left Clifford in Phoebe's care. Then Hepzibah would work at the counter in the shop while it was Phoebe's turn to be Clifford's nurse or caretaker.

Left on his own, Clifford would have sat indoors in his armchair from morning to night, but Phoebe managed to get him to go into the garden where she read aloud to him with her sweet, musical voice.

Clifford Seemed to Grow Younger.

Clifford enjoyed the flowers in the garden. He would hold one in his hand for hours, staring at its beauty and smelling its fragrance. At times he seemed unable to believe the happiness he was feeling. He would reach out to Phoebe, saying, "Take my hand, child, and pinch it hard with your little fingers so I might feel pain. Then I will know I'm not imagining the beauty here… that it is real… that the garden is real… and even this weather-beaten old house and Hepzibah's scowls are real!"

Having been locked away in prison for thirty years, gentle Clifford couldn't bear to see even the hens locked in their coop. So he insisted that Phoebe free them and let them roam, clucking around the garden as they pleased.

On Sundays, after Phoebe returned from church, Hepzibah, Clifford and Phoebe would have two guests in the garden. One was the photographer, Mr. Holgrave, and the other was Uncle Venner, who came dressed in his Sunday clothes: a clean white shirt and a jacket with fewer patches than the one he wore during the week when he did his odd jobs.

Clifford enjoyed talking to Uncle Venner. With a man older than himself, Clifford felt much younger.

It was at these Sunday gatherings that a smiling, happy Clifford joined in conversations with the others, and showed a hint of the intelligence he had had in his youth.

But as the sun faded at the end of each day, so would the excitement fade from Clifford's eyes. He became moody and often cried out, "I want my happiness! I've waited for it for so long, for so many years!"

Sadly, the most happiness that Clifford Pyncheon could look forward to now were the Sunday afternoons with his faithful Hepzibah, his sweet Phoebe, the friendly Holgrave, and the wisdom of Uncle Venner the philosopher with the patches on his clothes.

"Clifford Isn't Ready to Leave the House."

CHAPTER 10

The Arched Window

One evening after Clifford had gone to bed, Phoebe and Hepzibah were in the study talking.

"The Sunday afternoons in the garden with us and Mr. Holgrave and Uncle Venner are not enough time for Clifford to be with people," Phoebe said. "He needs to understand that there is a world outside of Pyncheon House."

"But Clifford isn't ready to leave the house," the devoted Hepzibah protested.

"Then I shall take him up to the big arched window on the second floor at the front of the house, the one that opens onto that small balcony. He can watch people passing by day to day. He could do that without fear of being seen by curious people down below if he sat behind the curtains."

"That will be fine, but do not let him go out on the balcony. The floor is rotted and could be dangerous," Hepzibah warned.

This new pastime delighted the old man. He always managed to follow some person, or some activity, with eagerness and wide-eyed interest.

A horse-drawn carriage that picked up and dropped off passengers was unknown to Clifford before he was sent to prison. The noise of the railroad, only a few blocks away, brought the old man to his feet to see where the steam floating to the sky was coming from.

And there were sights that he did remember from his youth: the butcher's cart with its white canopy, the fish-monger's wagon with its familiar conch shell horn, the countryman's cart going door to door selling fruits and vegetables, the baker's wagon with bells announcing its arrival, and the water carriage passing by three times a day.

There Were Sights He Did Remember.

The old man's favorite entertainment, though, was the organ-grinder with his little monkey dressed in a red-and-green plaid suit and hat. One day, when the organ-grinder came walking down Pyncheon Street with the monkey on his shoulder, he spotted Clifford and Phoebe up at the arched window. He immediately stopped under the elm and began to turn the crank on his barrel organ, a painted box pushed through the street like a baby-carriage.

As the music started, little mechanical figures on top of the cabinet began to move. The cobbler fixed a shoe, the lady waved her fan, the blacksmith hammered a horseshoe, the soldier waved his sword, the schoolboy opened his book, the milkmaid milked her cow and the miser counted his piles of gold. All these actions were in rhythm with the organ music.

At the end of the performance, the monkey jumped down to his master's feet. He turned his little wrinkled face to the passersby and to the children who had gathered around him. He held out his little hat in one hand and the open palm of his other hand. With well-trained chirps, he made it clear he was asking for coins for his master's music.

At the organ-grinder's urging, the little monkey looked up to the window where Clifford and Phoebe were watching. Smiling happily, Phoebe threw down a shiny coin to the monkey.

Clifford was delighted with the music and enjoyed watching the moving toy figures. But after staring at the funny-looking little monkey for a few minutes, the old man became so upset by its strange appearance that he began to cry. Clifford only wanted to see beautiful things. Another day, a noisy parade marched down Pyncheon Street. The blaring music and the tramping footsteps passed the usually quiet House of the Seven Gables, making Clifford shudder and turn pale. With his legs trembling, he rose, terrified, from his chair and attempted to climb up onto the windowsill.

If Clifford had reached over the sill and onto the balcony, the troubled man might have jumped into the street or fallen through the

Phoebe and Hepzibah Pulled Him Back.

rotted balcony. Fortunately, Phoebe and Hepzibah managed to pull him back by his clothes.

Once they had him safely back in his chair, Hepzibah scolded her brother. "Clifford, Clifford, are you crazy?" she screamed.

Clifford sighed deeply. "I don't know. Perhaps if I had jumped I would have been killed. Or if I had survived, I might be a different man—a man as I used to be. That is something to hope for."

One Sunday morning, as church bells were rung throughout the town, Clifford sat at the window with Hepzibah. They were watching townspeople filling the street on the way to church, when they looked down and saw Phoebe walking out the front door of the house. She opened her green parasol and looked up, smiling and waving to her two cousins at the window.

After watching Phoebe until she turned the corner, Clifford turned to Hepzibah and asked, "Dear sister, do you ever go to church?"

"No, I haven't gone for many years," she replied.

Heaving a big sigh, Clifford said, "Do you think I could pray again if I were among other people praying in church?"

Hepzibah stared at her brother. His face seemed to take on a glow as if God had put it there as a reward for his loving religious thoughts. "Dear brother," she said eagerly, "if that would please you, then we shall go. I'm certain we could find a place to kneel and pray in church."

So Hepzibah and Clifford dressed themselves in the best of their faded, old-fashioned clothes and walked down the staircase together.

The moment they opened the front door they both felt they were finally out in the world, but with everyone's eyes on them! Although the air was warm and sunny, Clifford and Hepzibah began to shiver, afraid to take one step more.

"We cannot do it, Hepzibah!" cried Clifford.

She Opened Her Parasol.

"It is too late. We are like ghosts. We don't belong among living human beings. We belong only in this old house, to haunt it and to live with the curse on it. And besides, I look so horrible that I would frighten everyone around us on the street and in the church, and I would make children hide behind their mothers' skirts!"

Clifford and Hepzibah went back up into the dark hallway and closed the door. Once again inside the dark, dismal House of the Seven Gables, they felt like the prisoners they had become.

As they climbed back up the staircase, Hepzibah murmured, "After that breath of fresh air, this house seems ten times more dismal than before."

But Clifford, in his childlike ways, was content to return to his window and spend hours watching children play ball in the street or roll hoops on the sidewalk. The old man was so brought back to his own childhood, he would often take his clay pipe and blow soap bubbles, one of his favorite pastimes as a child.

Passersby would look up at the old man with the wild white hair. Some would stare impolitely, while others smiled pleasantly as they remembered their own young days. Still others would use their fingers or walking sticks to touch and burst Clifford's sparkling bubbles as they floated down.

One very large bubble sailed gracefully down and burst on the nose of a dignified-looking elderly gentleman who happened to be passing by. He looked up, first glaring angrily. Then, upon seeing the old man in the window, he put a practiced smile on his face.

"Aha, Cousin Clifford!" cried Judge Pyncheon, his voice filled with sarcasm. "Still blowing soap bubbles at your age?"

As for Clifford, a terrible trembling of fear came over him. The poor weak man was still horrified at the sight of his cousin, the strong-willed, hateful judge.

That Left Phoebe Free.

CHAPTER 11

Mr. Holgrave's Fascinating Past

During the long days of summer, Phoebe spent mornings and part of the afternoon with Clifford. By mid-afternoon the old man would grow tired. It wasn't physical exercise that did it, for the most he ever did was walk in the garden or pace a room indoors on a rainy day. Whatever it was, Clifford was so exhausted that he was usually asleep by mid-afternoon.

That left Phoebe free for the rest of the day and evening. She would take a walk in town or on the beach, or attend a lecture or a concert, or she would shop in the village.

The only person Phoebe knew who was close to her age was Mr. Holgrave. They talked every day in the garden or in the shop.

One day when they both were in the garden, the young man told Phoebe he was from a poor family and that he had had very little education. "I left school at a young age," he explained. "And now at the age of twenty-two, I look back at all the jobs I've worked at and I am sometimes amazed. I've been a schoolteacher, a salesman, an editor, and a seller of colognes. I studied dentistry, worked on a cargo ship and traveled through Europe. More recently, I gave lectures on hypnotism."

Phoebe was impressed, but even more so when he proved his skill by hypnotizing the rooster, Chanticleer, and immediately putting him to sleep!

Phoebe listened to Holgrave with fascination. When he had finished, she asked, "And have you finally decided that your present career as a photographer is to be your permanent one?"

He Hypnotized Chanticleer.

"I don't consider it my life's work," he replied. "I do it now just to support myself. If I find something else that pleases me more, and at which I can earn more money, then I'll do that."

Phoebe thought Holgrave was friendly enough to Clifford and Hepzibah and herself— but she often noticed him looking at them as if studying them. He seemed to show a curious interest in them, especially in Clifford.

"Do you think the old gentleman is happy?" Holgrave asked Phoebe one day.

"It is hard to say," she answered. "His moods change so quickly without any cause. No one knows what he is thinking. But we have to understand what great sorrow he has lived through."

"I wish I could see into his thoughts," said Holgrave. I see such puzzling differences between Judge Pyncheon and Clifford, two people from the same f a m i l y. But enough of such talk! You have brought a ray of sunshine into The House of the Seven Gables and, if I may say so, into my life as well."

"Why, thank you very much, Mr. Holgrave,"

said Phoebe, blushing. "But tell me, what made you come to live at Pyncheon House in the first place?"

"I am pursuing my studies here," he said.

"Your studies? His answer puzzled Phoebe.

"I am studying the history of this house and the terrible events involving old Colonel Pyncheon and the wizard Matthew Maule," he explained.

"But why?" Phoebe asked.

"So I can hate it more than I do now!" he exclaimed.

Holgrave's answer dismayed Phoebe, but it also aroused her curiosity. "Hate it? But why? I've heard the story of these two men from Cousin Hepzibah. She believes that all of the terrible things that have happened to the Pyncheons began with that quarrel with the man you call the wizard."

"I believe that too," Holgrave agreed. "I believe that all the Pyncheons who are descended from the colonel have been infected with one kind of madness or another… that is, all except you, Phoebe."

"My Story—of Alice Pyncheon."

Phoebe didn't know whether to laugh at Holgrave or be frightened of him. But she tried to make light of his words and asked, "Is this Pyncheon madness contagious?"

"Not for you, dear Phoebe Pyncheon. But do you remember the man you saw in my daguerreotype, the man you thought was old Colonel Pyncheon? Well, he is part of the Pyncheon family history I am writing about."

"Oh, do you write as well as make daguerreotypes?" she asked eagerly.

"Yes, I write for magazines. I am well known for my stories of humor as well as for those that bring my readers to tears. May I read you one of my stories?" Holgrave asked.

"Yes," said Phoebe, laughing, "if it isn't very long or very dull."

"I cannot promise how interesting you will find it, but let us sit here in the garden and I shall read you my story—of Alice Pyncheon."

CHAPTER 12

The Tragic Tale of Alice Pyncheon

"Alice Pyncheon's story began thirty-seven years after old Colonel Pyncheon's death," Holgrave began.

"There are three people in my story. One Gervayse Pyncheon, the colonel's grandson. He was the very same grandson who, as a boy, ran into the study the day of the great housewarming festivities and discovered the old colonel dead at his desk. At the time of my story, Gervayse was a handsome middle-aged man with a large family, living in The House of the Seven Gables.

"One of Gervayse's children was the beauti-

Gervayse Pyncheon

ful Alice, the second person in my story. Alice had gone to school in Europe, where she learned to play the harpsichord, which she did beautifully."

"And who is the third person in your story?" Phoebe asked.

"That would be young Matthew Maule, the grandson and namesake of the original Matthew Maule who owned this land and was put to death for being a wizard and practicing witch-craft, as you know," Holgrave said.

He continued. "Now, young Matthew Maule was a carpenter, just like his father, Thomas Maule. And it was Thomas who had built The House of the Seven Gables for the old colonel. The colonel knew that Thomas was the best carpenter in town, and wanted only Thomas to build the great mansion.

"One day, after Gervayse had returned after many years in Europe, he sent Scipio, one of his servants, to Matthew Maule, summoning him to Pyncheon House.

"'And what does your master want with me?' snapped the young carpenter. 'Perhaps thirty-seven years after my father built it, the roof needs some repairs?' " Holgrave read on.

"'The house is in good shape,' replied Scipio, 'except for the ghost of old Matthew Maule that haunts it.'

"'Well, tell your master that I'll be there when I finish what I'm doing. I'm glad that he appreciates that I'm the best carpenter in town, but my skills do not include keeping spirits from haunting The House of the Seven Gables.'

"As Scipio turned to go, Matthew Maule added, 'If you happen to see the lovely Mistress Alice, tell her Matthew Maule asked about her.'

"Now, this young Matthew Maule was not very well liked in town, even though people couldn't say anything bad about his skill or his hard work or his honesty. The dislike was more because he was the grandson of Matthew Maule, who everyone believed was a wizard.

"The wizard, who was one of the early settlers of the town, was among many people who had been charged with witchcraft and hanged. Legends say that old Matthew Maule haunted

Maule's Ghost Haunted the House.

The House of the Seven Gables as a ghost, afterward, because he was the original owner of the land where that house now stands, and because Colonel Pyncheon had cheated him out of it.

"Maule's ghost insisted, just as Matthew Maule did when he was alive, that he was the rightful owner and that rent money should be paid to him from the day that the cellar was first dug, and that the mansion should be given to him.

"The threat was that if this weren't done, Maule's ghost would make everything go wrong for the Pyncheons, even for a thousand years after the wizard's death.

"In addition, the younger Matthew Maule was believed by many to have inherited his grandfather's powers of witchcraft. He was supposed to be able to get into people's minds—especially those of young women—and get them to do as he ordered. They called it the 'Witchcraft of Maule's Eye.'

"After young Matthew received Gervayse

Pyncheon's message from the servant Scipio, he returned to the job he was working on until it was finished. Only then did he set off for The House of the Seven Gables.

"People had always heard that the present owner of Pyncheon House, Gervayse Pyncheon, disliked the mansion ever since the day when, as a child, he had run to his grandfather in the study, only to discover that the old colonel was dead! As a result, Gervayse Pyncheon lived much of his adult life in Europe, letting a distant relative live in the house.

"As young Matthew Maule approached The House of the Seven Gables, he mused to himself, 'I guess the Pyncheon relative kept the house in good order. The roof looks good and the peaks of the gables are sharp, and the outside walls have no breaks in their plaster.'

"Matthew looked up at one of the open windows on the second story and spotted a beautiful young lady there. The sight of Alice Pyncheon brought a smile to the young carpenter's eager face.

Matthew Spotted a Beautiful Young Lady.

"Then his eyes were drawn to a sundial on the front gable. 'Three o'clock,' he muttered. 'My father told me that the sundial was put up only an hour before the colonel's death, and that has kept accurate time for thirty-seven years.'

"It was proper for a workman like Matthew Maule to enter a gentleman's mansion through the back door, which servants and other workers used. But the carpenter was a stubborn young man, a bitter young man, because he considered the Pyncheon house to be standing on his land.

"So, young Matthew strode directly to the front door and banged loudly with the heavy iron knocker. 'Here I am!' he announced when Scipio opened the door. 'Show me to your master!'

"As Matthew stepped inside the house, sweet music filled the hallway from an upstairs room. It was the harpsichord that Alice Pyncheon had brought with her from Europe. Gervayse Pyncheon had been impatiently waiting for Matthew Maule, so Scipio brought the young man into his master's study immediately.

"The study was filled with beautiful furniture and works of art from Europe, mingled with a few pieces of original furniture from the old colonel's time. Only two items seemed out of place. One was a large map of a piece of land. The map was dirtied with fingerprints and yellowed with age. The other was a portrait of a stern old man wearing clothes of a Puritan settler, with a sword in one hand and a Bible in the other—the portrait of old Colonel Pyncheon.

"Matthew Maule looked at the elegantly dressed middle-aged man seated at a desk near the fire. Matthew then, without waiting to be invited in, walked to the hearth and turned to face Gervayse Pyncheon.

"'You sent for me,' said the carpenter. 'Please explain what you want so I can get back to my own work.'

"'Forgive me,' said Gervayse quietly. 'I did not mean to take up your time without payment. Your name is Maule, isn't it? You are the

"I Am Well Aware of the Dispute."

son, or is it grandson, of the Maule who built this house?'

"'I am Matthew Maule, the son of the man who built this house and the grandson of the rightful owner of this land.'

"'I am well aware of the dispute between your grandfather and mine,' said Gervayse. 'I know that the colonel went to court to get this land, and even though the ownership was decided in my grandfather's favor, I can understand why you walked in here resenting me. But I think we can discuss how you and I can settle this dispute fairly, for both our benefits.'

"The carpenter's anger seemed to decrease. 'Go on,' he said.

"'You are probably aware that over the years, my family has been trying to settle a claim to a very large piece of land to the east.' Then Gervayse Pyncheon pointed to the old map on the study wall.

"Matthew smiled. 'Yes, I've heard about that very often from my father.'

"Gervayse Pyncheon looked at Matthew's smiling face and hoped his words were well received as he went on. 'At the time of my grandfather's death, he had the deed to these Eastern Lands in his possession. His friends and business associates knew about it. But then the deed disappeared.'

"A smile of satisfaction crossed Matthew's face as he said, 'But what can a poor carpenter have to do with the business affairs of the great Pyncheon family?'

"'Perhaps nothing, Mr. Maule, or possibly much! You see, both our grandfathers had been negotiating for the land to the east and had agreed upon a deal. Everyone knew that your grandfather had got the better end of the deal since he received the great Eastern Territory in exchange for the two acres where this house now sits. But the original deed giving the Pyncheons the Eastern Lands has never been found.'

"'I still don't see what—' the carpenter interrupted.

"'Let me finish, Mr. Maule,' Gervayse went on. 'I was a child when my grandfather died, but

"But Then the Deed Disappeared."

I do remember that your father was doing some work in this very room on the morning of the old colonel's death. And I also remember seeing some papers spread out on my grandfather's desk.'

"'Are you accusing my father of stealing the deed just to get those Eastern Lands back again?' cried Matthew angrily. 'My father was more honest than your bloody old colonel!'

"'I will not get into an argument with a workman like you,' Gervayse snapped. 'I am a gentleman and a businessman, and I will pay you for any information you can give me to help me find the lost deed, which is my rightful claim to the land.'

"'Tell me, Mr. Pyncheon, if I agree to give you the information you need, would you pay me by giving me back my grandfather's land, together with this House of the Seven Gables on it?'

"All during this conversation, the portrait of old Colonel Pyncheon seemed to be behaving strangely. The old man's frown deepened and his fists clenched when Matthew Maule suggested returning Pyncheon House and its land to the Maule family. The portrait seemed to have lost all patience and the colonel's body appeared ready to step out of the picture and into the room.

"The two men were too involved in their conversation to look up and notice anything. But it must be noted here that the legend says that if that portrait were ever taken down, the entire House of the Seven Gables would come thundering down to ruin.

"'Give up this house and its land!' cried Gervayse in horror. 'If I did that, my grandfather would come back from the grave!'

"'That is your concern, not mine,' said Matthew Maule. 'I have no other to offer.'

"Although Gervayse reacted angrily at first to Matthew Maule's offer, he then thought to himself, I have no real feelings for this house or for my childhood spent here. In fact, I cannot forget that ghastly morning when I found my grandfather dead behind his desk in this very room. Besides, after all the years I've

"I Could Perhaps Become an Earl."

spent in Europe, in castles in England and palaces in Italy, I feel nothing but contempt for this dreary House of the Seven Gables. Unfortunately I was forced to return here when I used up all of my dead wife's fortune, plus practically all of my Pyncheon fortune as well.

"Of course, Matthew Gervayse continued reasoning to himself, with those Eastern Lands, I would be a wealthy man and could even buy an important title back in England, perhaps become an earl, or a lord. Certainly, I couldn't buy such grandeur if I were simply the owner of seven ugly gables!

"But Gervayse Pyncheon took care not to let the young Matthew Maule read his thoughts. And he had to keep from laughing in the carpenter's face at the offer of such easy terms to get the land he desperately wanted.

"'I agree to your deal, Maule,' Gervayse finally said. 'You get me the deed I need to prove I am the owner of those lands, and The House of the Seven Gables is yours.' Gervayse looked at the portrait of his grandfather and caught his breath. Did I see the old colonel frowning at me? he wondered.

"'And now, sir, if you wish information about the lost document, I must ask first for a few minutes to talk with your beautiful daughter, Alice,' Matthew stated.

"'You are mad, Maule!' Gervayse snarled. 'My daughter has nothing to do with this business!'

"Alice's music came floating from upstairs, accompanied by her sweet singing.

"Gervayse thought, I can understand why Maule wants the house and land beneath it. But I am completely bewildered at his reasons for asking to see Alice.

"'I insist, Pyncheon!' Matthew demanded. 'I can only locate the lost papers through Alice. If you refuse, we have no deal!'

"Gervayse was not about to let go of such valuable lands over a few minutes of conversation with his daughter, so he sent a servant to call her down to the study.

"As Alice walked into the study, her eyes fell upon the carpenter. Matthew was in his

"I Must Talk with Your Daughter Alice."

work clothes, with a bandanna sticking out of the deep pocket in his trousers. A wide smile crossed her face and her eyes sparkled admiringly at the good-looking young carpenter.

"Any man would have been delighted to have such a beautiful young woman smile at him, but Matthew just gritted his teeth and mumbled under his breath. 'Look at her. She is so proud and aristocratic. So vain! But she may not be that way for long!'

"Alice turned to her father. 'You sent for me, but if you have business with this young man, I'll go. I do not like being in this room.'

"'Stay a moment, Miss Pyncheon,' said Matthew. 'My business with your father is finished. However, my business with you now begins.'

"Alice turned to her father, puzzled.

"'Yes, Alice,' Gervayse Pyncheon said. 'This young man claims he can locate a lost document through you. And it is essential that I find it. I do not understand it, but please cooperate with Mr. Maule and answer his questions.

I will stay here with you so you do not have to worry about being alone with him. If at any time you wish to end this, we will stop.'

"'I am not afraid of this man and certainly not with my father here!' Alice said. She had no way of knowing what she was about to experience.

"'Then, Mistress Alice,' said Matthew, 'please sit down and simply stare into my eyes!'

"Alice was proud of the power her beauty gave her, and she believed she was in full control of this common workman.

"Gervayse stood with his eyes on a painting on the wall, but he did not really see the scene on the canvas. His mind was haunted with the tales of mysterious supernatural powers that the Maules were said to possess. Perhaps that power had even been given to the grandson here!

"Gervayse had lived in Europe for so many years, he had almost pushed those tales out of his mind, but now, they were all coming back to

149

"Oh Father, I Am Fine."

him. Hadn't Matthew Maule been proven guilty of witchcraft? Hadn't he passed the hatred of the Pyncheons down to his son? Had his grandson received that hatred as well? Was Matthew now going to try to practice witchcraft on Alice?

"Gervayse turned around to see Matthew Maule with his arms up in the air as if pressing an invisible weight down on Alice's head. 'Stop, Maule!' Gervayse cried. 'I forbid you to go any further!'

"'Oh, Father,' Alice said, sitting and staring straight ahead. 'What he is doing is harmless. I am fine, truly I am.'

"Gervayse turned back to the painting and didn't interrupt again. After all, wasn't he doing it because his beautiful daughter would then have a rich dowry and could marry an English earl or a prince instead of some New England lawyer or clergyman?

"At one point, Gervayse heard a weak cry from his daughter. Was it a call for help? He was so filled with his illusions of wealth, he did not even turn around.

"After a while, Matthew spoke. 'Look, Pyncheon, look at your daughter!'

"Gervayse Pyncheon turned around and quickly came to the side of his daughter's chair.

"Matthew was in front of Alice pointing at her as she sat with her eyes tightly closed. His face glowed with triumph as he announced, 'There she is! Speak to her!'

"'Alice! My daughter!' Gervayse cried.

"The girl didn't move.

"'Louder!' said Matthew, smiling.

"'Alice, wake up!' her father shouted. 'It worries me to see you like this. Wake up!'

"By now, Gervayse was screaming in terror, but his voice didn't reach his daughter.

"'Try to touch her,' said Maule. 'Shake her.'

"Gervayse took Alice's hand and pressed it. He kissed her. Getting no response, he shook her again. Finally, he let go of her and she fell back limp against her chair.

"'Villain!' shouted Gervayse, shaking h i s fists in a terrified rage. 'You have robbed me

"There She Is! Speak to Her!"

of my daughter! Give her back to me or go to the gallows in your grandfather's footsteps!'

"'Speak softly, Mr. Pyncheon, and do not shake your fists at me,' said Maule scornfully. 'Is it my crime if you sold your daughter for a piece of yellow paper? Your daughter sits quietly asleep. Now, I will see if she is as proud and confident as she was earlier.'

"Matthew murmured some words to Alice, and she replied with a nod as she leaned toward him. He beckoned to her. She rose from her chair and walked toward him. He then waved her back and she sank into her chair.

"'She is mine!' Matthew shouted, with an evil laugh. 'Mine! I have complete power over her!'

"The legend says that his idea had been to enter Alice's mind, and through it to make contact with the spirits of the old colonel and Matthew and Thomas Maule, who knew where the lost document was.

"According to legend, while in the trance, Alice described in detail seeing the three men.

She even told of seeing the bloodstain on the colonel's hand as he held the now missing deed, refusing to give it to Maule.

"At this point, the young carpenter said to Gervayse, 'That document will stay lost until it no longer has any value. You must keep The House of the Seven Gables and its curse!'

"Gervayse tried to speak, but the only sound coming from his throat was a gurgle!

"Matthew smiled. 'Aha!' he cried. 'There's the curse! You have old Maule's blood to drink!'

"'You are the devil!' Pyncheon raged. 'Give me back my daughter. I never want to see you again!'

"'Your daughter!' Matthew sneered. 'She is mine, she is in my power. But I will leave her with you. She will never remember Maule the carpenter!'

"Matthew waved his hands in the air several times. Alice awoke from her trance. After a few moments, she seemed to regain her dignity. The beautiful young girl had no idea that an unknown power had taken possession of her

155

All He Had to Do Was Wave His Hand.

will, that she would be the victim of his terrible control.

"This power was so strong that even when Matthew was at home, all he had to do was wave his hand and no matter where Alice was—in her home, at church, or out with friends—she instantly came under his power. If he said, 'Alice, laugh!' or even thought it, Alice would break into laughter whether she was in the middle of saying prayers in church, or weeping at a funeral.

"It was not his intention to harm her but to make her the object of ridicule. This would take away the aristocratic pride from her life, and the power she believed she had because of her beauty.

"One evening, Alice was at a wedding— not hers, for she felt it would be a sin to marry when she had no control over her life. While at the wedding, she was ordered by Matthew to go to a workingman's crude home. So, in her pretty party gown and satin slippers, Alice hurried to the house where Matthew's own bride was preparing for her wedding. He sent Alice there as a servant to wait on his bride.

"It was a terrible night with fierce winds driving rain and snow into her thin dress, and mud from the streets filled her soft slippers.

"The next day, Alice came down with a cold and cough that didn't go away. She lingered for several weeks as her body weakened and wasted away. But she loved her music, and on the day before she died, Alice played her harpsichord so sadly, as if to say that there would be a death in the Pyncheon family.

"Alice Pyncheon's funeral was the grandest the town had ever seen, and the mourners' procession was the longest.

"At the end of the long line of mourners came Matthew, gnashing his teeth, sadly muttering to himself, 'What have I done? I only wanted to humble Alice, not kill her. I took her sweet, delicate soul into my power for my own selfish pride, and now she's dead.'"

It Was a Terrible Night.

CHAPTER 13

Phoebe's Good-bye

Holgrave had read his story with such drama and energy, describing Matthew Maule's arm-waving movements, that when he was finished he noticed Phoebe seemed drowsy, as her eyelids closed over her eyes.

As Holgrave rolled up the pages of his manuscript, he gazed at Phoebe. He realized he had actually created in her the beginnings of a hypnotic trance. Holgrave knew that with one wave of his hand he could completely overpower Phoebe, much as Matthew Maule had done with Alice Pyncheon in his story!

But instead he made a slight gesture

upward with his hand. Smiling half-sarcastically he said, "You really offend me, Miss Phoebe. If my poor story was so dull as to make you fall asleep, it will never do for me to submit it to a magazine where the critics will be merciless. I'd better just use my manuscript to light the flames in my fireplace."

"Me, asleep?" Phoebe replied, completely unaware how close she was to having been hypnotized by Holgrave. "No, sir. I was really quite attentive. I do remember very well how much trouble and tragedy occurred in your story."

By this time, evening had come, with the moon casting shadows on the garden. Phoebe rose from the bench.

"I must go in and help Cousin Hepzibah with the figures from today's sales in the shop. She is not very quick with numbers and they give her a headache."

"I heard from Miss Hepzibah that in a few days you are returning to your home in the country," Holgrave said.

"I am only going for a short while to make a few arrangements and say good-bye to my

"That House Is No Longer My Home."

mother and my friends," Phoebe replied. "That house is no longer my home. Pyncheon House is my true home now. It is where I am wanted and needed and loved."

"Yes, you are, Phoebe, more than you can imagine," Holgrave said warmly. "You have brought sunshine and life into this house, and I fear both will vanish when you leave. Miss Hepzibah has cut herself off from all life outside The House of the Seven Gables. She considers herself alive when she stands in her shop and scowls at people. Her poor brother Clifford has just about been brought back from the dead. They are both somewhat alive only because of you!"

"I would hate to think that about them. I take great interest in their welfare. As for you, Mr. Holgrave, I sometimes wonder whether you wish them well or wish them ill. Are you their friend or their enemy?" she asked bluntly.

Holgrave spoke in a strange tone. "I am interested in this poverty-stricken old lady and this shattered gentleman. They are helpless old

163

children. I am watching a drama being played, one that began two hundred years ago on this very ground where we stand. But I have a feeling this drama will end soon."

Holgrave's words puzzled and angered Phoebe. "How can you call Hepzibah and Clifford's misfortunes a drama? They are not actors on a stage. This old house is not a theater! Clifford and Hepzibah are real and deeply hurt. They are old people. And you, who see yourself as their audience, are cold-hearted and unfeeling!"

"Your words are cruel," Holgrave protested.

"I'm not finished, Mr. Holgrave! What do you mean the drama will end soon? Do you know of any new troubles hanging over my poor cousins? You must tell me!"

"Forgive me, Miss Phoebe," said Holgrave. "I must confess that I sometimes think I am a mystic, that I can see into the future, along with my ability to hypnotize. Believe me, if I knew of any secret that would harm your cousins, who truly are my friends, I would tell you but I have

"They Are Not Actors on a Stage."

no such knowledge."

"But still I sense that you are holding something back," Phoebe insisted.

"No, nothing, only my personal secrets," replied Holgrave. "I do notice, however, that Judge Pyncheon has been keeping his eye on Clifford. I am also aware that the judge had a lot to do with sending Clifford to jail. Why he did it and why he is so interested in the old man now, I have no idea. What can such a wealthy and powerful judge possibly fear from a man like Clifford? Yet I believe that if he could have Clifford killed, he would."

"You speak as if something terrible is going to happen!" Phoebe cried.

"No, no, Miss Phoebe," Holgrave protested, taking her hand. "Sometimes I get into these dark moods. Everyone does—except you, dear Phoebe. You are always so full of happiness and sunshine. But please, let us part as friends, or at least before you begin to hate me."

CHAPTER 14

Judge Jaffrey Pyncheon's Threat

Several days passed after Phoebe's departure. They were dreary days from a storm that blew in from the sea. Indoors at Pyncheon House, they were dreary as well. Clifford was cut off from the enjoyment of sitting at the arched window, watching people go by. He couldn't go out into the garden, which was muddy.

As for Hepzibah, she spent time in the shop, but very few customers came in. It seems that someone had spread a rumor all around the town that her scowl spoiled her cooked goods.

Throughout the four stormy days, Hepzibah kept Clifford company in the study as

The Visitor Was Judge Jaffrey Pyncheon.

much as possible.

The house was quiet, but one day Hepzibah heard sounds from upstairs. It was music!

"It is Alice Pyncheon's harpsichord," she whispered to herself. "Clifford must be playing. Could the music be announcing a Pyncheon death now, just as it did the last time Mistress Alice played it?"

Then suddenly, after a few notes, the music stopped. The loud tinkling of the shop's bell distracted Hepzibah from her fears. Heavy footsteps could be heard entering the shop.

Hepzibah drew her shawl around her and headed toward the shop. Before she reached the door, she heard a gurgling sound coming from the chest of the visitor who had entered.

Hepzibah's fears turned to anger. The visitor was Judge Jaffrey Pyncheon.

"How do you do, Cousin Hepzibah," said the judge. "I tried the front door but it was locked. So I came in through the shop instead.

And how is this terrible weather affecting our poor Clifford? I am most concerned. I came to see if I can help make him or you more comfortable."

"I take care of Clifford myself and he has everything he needs," Hepzibah snapped.

"I'm sure you do, dear Cousin, but you keep him so secluded. That cannot be good for him. Why, if I can see Clifford now, I will prove to you how good it will make him feel."

"No! You cannot see him! He has been ill in bed since yesterday."

"Ill? Ill? Then I must and will see him! What if he should die?" he cried in a panic.

"He is not in danger of dying," said Hepzibah, "unless he is persecuted by the very same man who so cruelly persecuted him thirty years ago! You, Jaffrey Pyncheon!"

"Cousin Hepzibah," said the judge, appearing to be hurt by the old woman's words, "you have no idea how unfair and unkind your accusations are. I was forced by the law to do what I did to Clifford. But I had to do my duty.

"I Take Care of Clifford!"

My actions have caused me pain all these years. I have cried along with you at his fate. But now he is free. We shall both devote ourselves to making him happy. I am not your enemy. Let me prove it."

"You and your lying tongue can prove nothing to me!" Hepzibah shouted. "I know you better! You only pretend to care about Clifford! Say it! Be a man! You have some evil motive behind your false words of kindness and love. Don't ever speak those words to me again!"

Hepzibah's outrage had given her the courage to speak this way to Judge Pyncheon, to defy this prominent and powerful man who was respected by everyone.

Everyone, that is, except Hepzibah, some of the judge's political enemies, and perhaps Mr. Holgrave.

Of course, when Jaffrey Pyncheon was alone and looked in the mirror, sometimes he would remember his reckless youth. But he always managed to push his evil deeds out of his mind and concentrate on his present good deeds.

During Hepzibah's violent outburst, the judge faced his cousin with a look of patience and a smile. But when Hepzibah was finished, he turned a hard, scowling face to her.

Hepzibah stared at him as a sudden realization came to her. My God! she thought to herself. He's the exact image of the portrait of old Colonel Pyncheon!

Then the judge spoke firmly. "Cousin Hepzibah, it is time to end all this."

"I agree," said Hepzibah. "So stop persecuting us. Leave us in peace. That's all we want."

But that wasn't what Jaffrey Pyncheon wanted. "I intend to see Clifford before I leave this house," he insisted, "so stop behaving like a madwoman, Hepzibah. I am Clifford's only friend and a powerful one at that. Are you so blind that you cannot see that it was only through my efforts and my political influence that Clifford was freed from prison? Did you really think that his release meant you had won over me? No, my good cousin, I set him free!"

"I Was the One Who Set Him Free."

"I don't believe it!" cried Hepzibah. "I'll never believe it. You put him in prison, but it was God's will that freed my brother and brought him back to me!"

"No, Hepzibah, I was the one who set him free," said the judge calmly. "And I came here to decide whether he shall stay free or not. It depends on him, and that's why I must see him."

"Never! It would drive him mad! And why would you want to see this wretched man, who is half out of his mind, but will never show that to anybody but those who love him?"

"He shall see love from me," said the judge with complete confidence. "But please, listen a moment and I will explain why I must see him."

Hepzibah stood with her arms folded across her chest. The judge ignored her and went on.

"Thirty years ago, at our Uncle Jaffrey's death, no one knew how wealthy he was because he was somewhat eccentric. He had made many investments. Because he was so strange, he made them under other names."

"So what does that have to do with us now?" Hepzibah demanded.

"In Uncle Jaffrey's will, as you are aware, his entire estate was left to me—with the single exception of Pyncheon House and its land for you and your brother to live in during your lifetime."

"And do you intend to take that away from us?" Hepzibah snapped. "Is that your price for leaving us alone?"

"Certainly not, my dear cousin," answered the judge, his face all smiles, as usual. "I have reason to believe that Clifford might give me a clue as to what happened to the greater part of Uncle Jaffrey's money. It was never found after his death."

"Clifford!" exclaimed Hepzibah. "You really think that Clifford knows about hidden wealth? That he has any power whatsoever to make you rich? It is laughable to even think that!"

"I am as certain of it as I am that I'm standing here," said the judge, stamping his foot and his cane on the floor to emphasize his point. "Besides, Clifford told me so himself."

"Is That Your Price?"

"No! No! You are dreaming, Cousin Jaffrey," Hepzibah insisted.

"I am not a person who dreams or makes up stories," the judge said firmly. "A few months before our uncle's death, Clifford boasted to me that he knew a secret about great wealth. He was trying to tease me, but I do believe he spoke the truth. Clifford can tell me where to find the documents or whatever evidence exists to lead me to Uncle Jaffrey's missing property."

"But why would Clifford have kept it a secret for so long?" asked Hepzibah.

"He believed I was his enemy and the cause of his imprisonment, of course. And while he was there, he surely didn't want to see me get any wealthier. But the time has come for him to reveal his secret," the judge stated.

"And if he refuses? Or—as I truly believe—he has no knowledge of this wealth after all?" Hepzibah asked.

"My dear Cousin Hepzibah," said Judge Pyncheon in a threatening tone, "since your brother's return, I have made it my business to have him watched. I have had reports from neighbors, from passersby who saw his strange behavior when he tried to jump into the street and many other times. I myself even saw him blowing bubbles from the window. Quite a strange pastime for a man his age, wouldn't you say?" the judge taunted. He paused, but Hepzibah didn't answer.

"From all these stories, I am led to believe that Clifford is so insane, he cannot be permitted to stay free. I fear that as a judge, I shall have to make the decision to send him to a public lunatic asylum, where he shall have to live for the rest of his life."

"You cannot mean that!" Hepzibah shrieked.

"Oh, but I do," said the judge quite calmly. "If Cousin Clifford refuses to give me the information I demand and which I know he does possess, I shall consider it an example of his insanity. And you know, Cousin Hepzibah, that I will do what I said I would."

"Talk Sense, Hepzibah!"

"Oh, Cousin Jaffrey," cried Hepzibah mournfully. "It is you who are insane, not Clifford. You are an old man with not that many more years to live. Aren't you rich enough? You'll never be hungry, you'll never be without fancy clothes, or worry about a roof over your head. With half of what you have, you could afford expensive food and wine, and a house twice as big as the one you live in, and still have riches to leave to your son. Why are you doing this cruel, cruel thing? You are carrying on the wicked ways of your ancestors and sending down that curse you inherited!"

"Talk sense, Hepzibah!" the judge snapped back, losing his patience. "My mind is made up. I will not change it. Clifford must give up his secret or suffer for it. And he must decide quickly. I have several important appointments this morning and a special dinner this evening."

"Clifford has no secrets," Hepzibah said. "God will not let you do this."

"We shall see," said the judge firmly. "Now decide. Will you call Clifford and we settle this in a friendly way as cousins should or shall I resort to harsher measures? It is entirely up to you, Hepzibah."

"You are stronger than I am, Cousin Jaffrey, but your strength has no pity. Clifford is not insane, but the meeting you insist on will surely drive him to insanity. Knowing you as I do, I think it is best for you to judge for yourself if my brother knows any valuable secret. I will call him. Please be gentle with him and remember, Jaffrey Pyncheon, God is watching you!"

The judge followed Hepzibah from the shop into the study. He flung himself into the great armchair of his ancestors, the chair in which old Colonel Pyncheon had been found dead.

And now, with the old colonel frowning down at him from his portrait, the judge took his watch from his vest pocket and waited impatiently for Clifford to appear.

He Flung Himself into the Chair.

CHAPTER 15

A Frightening Discovery!

As Hepzibah slowly climbed the creaking stairs on her heartbreaking errand, she gazed around in fear. The terrible scene she had just struggled through with her Cousin Jaffrey left her shattered and shaking with panic.

"He is just like the old Colonel Pyncheon," she sobbed, as each step brought her closer to Clifford's room. "And now we will be adding more sadness to the family history! But I am not interested in family history. I care only about the pain this will cause Clifford. He is so fragile now from his past misfortunes, he will be completely broken, at having to face the man

184

who has been the one evil force in his life."

No matter how slowly she dragged her steps, Hepzibah finally reached Clifford's door and knocked weakly.

There was no reply!

She knocked again, a little harder.

Still no response!

Hepzibah called her brother's name, thinking he was in a sound sleep with his head buried in the pillows and the covers pulled over his head. Or possibly he had heard Jaffrey's voice from downstairs and was refusing to answer the knock.

Finally, she turned the knob and entered Clifford's room.

It was empty!

Hepzibah hurried to the window to see if perhaps Clifford was in the garden. He was not.

Hepzibah's mind began to race, trying to imagine what might have happened to her brother. Could Clifford have heard the judge talking and escaped into the street? But then he would be ridiculed as he roamed the town, rambling on and on with his foolish talk.

"You Must Help Me Find Him!"

This was too much for Hepzibah. Jaffrey Pyncheon must help her! She hurried down the staircase, shrieking, "Clifford is gone! I cannot find him! I fear he will be hurt!"

Hepzibah flung open the study door. In the darkened room, she could barely make out the judge seated in the old armchair.

"Clifford is not in his bedroom!" she shrieked. "You must help me find him!"

Judge Jaffrey Pyncheon was not the type of man who panicked in an emergency situation. That would have been beneath his dignity. So he just sat there, never bothering to answer Hepzibah.

"Don't you hear me, Jaffrey Pyncheon?" Hepzibah screamed. "Clifford is gone!"

At that moment there was a sudden movement behind Hepzibah. It was Clifford, coming from behind the door she had flung open. On his face was an expression of joy and excitement as he jumped in front of her and pointed his shaking fingers into the darkened room.

"Hush! Hush, Clifford! Has our evil cousin's visit driven you completely out of your mind?" she whispered. "Do not speak, dear brother, for Judge Jaffrey is sitting here and quietly studying you."

"Let him be quiet!" Clifford answered, pointing behind him. "As for us, now we can dance and sing. We can laugh and play. We can do whatever we want! The weight is gone! The evil is gone! We can now be as happy and carefree as little Phoebe herself."

Suddenly a terrible fear gripped Hepzibah. She pushed past Clifford into the room. A horrifying cry choked in her throat. The figure seated in the armchair and still holding his watch did not move, did not speak, did not breathe.

Judge Pyncheon was dead!

Hepzibah turned back to see Clifford trembling from head to foot. Was it joy or fear?

"My God!" she cried. "What will happen to us?"

"Come!" Clifford ordered in a strong, powerful voice that surprised Hepzibah. "We have

"We Can Be Happy!"

stayed here too long. Let us leave this house to our Cousin Jaffrey. He will take good care of it."

Full of horror at what she had seen, Hepzibah froze. She was afraid to ask her brother, or even imagine, how it had all happened. When she finally tore her eyes away from the corpse in the chair, she saw that her brother was now wearing his old cloak, the one he always had on during heavy New England storms.

"What are you waiting for, dear sister?" Clifford asked. "Put on your cloak and gather your purse. Take whatever money you have and let us go!"

Hepzibah obeyed. She hurried upstairs, still trying to decide if she was dreaming or if a dead Jaffrey Pyncheon was really seated in the old colonel's study.

"Now I shall wake up," she murmured as she began following Clifford's instructions. "I cannot bear this. I must wake up now!"

But this was no dream for Hepzibah—not even on the way out of the house when Clifford stopped at the study doorway and made a low, theatrical bow to the dead man in the armchair. Then he whispered to his sister, "What an absurd sight Jaffrey Pyncheon is now! Just when he thought he had me in his clutches! Come, Hepzibah, let us hurry before his ghost rises up and catches us."

Clifford and Hepzibah left The House of the Seven Gables and left Judge Jaffrey Pyncheon behind, in the home of his ancestors—all by himself, still staring with eyes that did not see the watch ticking in his hand, a watch that ticked away the seconds of his wicked plans that were now never to happen.

At the Railroad Station

CHAPTER 16

Fleeing and Wandering

Even though it was summer, Hepzibah's teeth chattered as she and Clifford hurried up Pyncheon Street toward the center of town. A heavy rain was falling, but it didn't slow the elderly pair. It was as if two inexperienced children were on an expedition to the ends of the earth.

As Hepzibah cast a fearful, sidelong glance at Clifford, she saw a powerful excitement in his movements. His smile was one of triumph.

They made their way to the railroad station, where a train with two passenger cars was ready to leave. Clifford helped Hepzibah up into one of the cars and climbed up behind her.

Hepzibah was unable to believe what was happening. She murmured to her brother, "Clifford, am I dreaming?"

"No, dear Hepzibah," Clifford replied with a chuckle. "It is not a dream. I have never been more awake in my life than I am now!"

They settled down in their seats in the railroad car. The novelty of being enclosed under one long narrow roof with fifty other people fascinated them.

They stared at the travelers who were engrossed in their newspapers, or books. They watched a few young people tossing a ball across the aisle. They followed the progress of food-sellers who came aboard at each station, peddling their apples, cakes and candy. They looked intently as each new person entered and left. This was a world Hepzibah and Clifford had never known!

Clifford was delighted to watch life coming and going around him. But Hepzibah huddled in the corner of her seat, feeling even more alone than she did at Pyncheon House.

"Am I Dreaming?"

"You are not happy, Hepzibah," Clifford scolded. "You are thinking of that dismal house and Cousin Jaf-" Clifford shuddered before he could get the name out. But after a moment, he went on. "Of course, you are thinking of Cousin Jaffrey sitting there all by himself. Forget that, dear sister. We are here now, in the midst of life. We are with people! Let us be happy, as happy as those young people tossing that ball about."

Happy! Hepzibah thought bitterly. He is truly mad! If I were fully awake, I'd probably go mad too!

As the train clattered along the iron tracks, Hepzibah stared bleakly out the window. But she didn't see the towns and villages passing by. All she could see was Pyncheon Street... and The House of the Seven Gables... and the shop... and a customer maybe shaking the door and jingling the bell fiercely without disturbing Judge Pyncheon!

Hepzibah feared she was too set in her ways to let new things enter her mind as Clifford could. At home she was his guardian.

Here, Clifford had become her guide, and he had done it with speed and intelligence.

The conductor came by for tickets and Clifford put a bill in his hand as he had seen other people do.

"How far are you going?" asked the conductor.

"As far as that money will take us," answered Clifford pleasantly. "We are riding for our enjoyment today."

An old gentleman across the aisle looked up from his newspaper and commented, "You have chosen a strange day for pleasure riding with this storm outside. The greatest enjoyment on such a day is to be at home with a nice warm fire in the chimney."

"I cannot agree with you," said Clifford, nodding courteously to the man. "I believe that this wonderful invention, the railroad, will change people's ideas of enjoyment and pleasure."

Having found a gentleman with whom to have a conversation, Clifford spent the better part of the next hour in an interesting discussion with the man across the aisle. Clifford's

It Surprised the Other Passengers.

voice was now the voice of a youthful, active gentleman. It surprised the other passengers to hear it come from a man with white hair and pale, wrinkled skin. Many of them stopped what they were doing to stare at him.

One woman whispered to her husband, "That man must have captured many a woman's heart when he was young!"

When the conversation between the gentleman and Clifford touched on the subject of homes, Clifford commented bitterly, "My dingy and rusty old house holds only memories of death for me! I shall never set foot in The House of the Seven Gables again! The farther away from it I get, the more my youth and its joys come back to me."

"For Heaven's sake, Clifford, be quiet!" Hepzibah whispered. "They'll think you are mad!"

"Be quiet yourself!" Clifford snapped. "I don't care what they think. I am not mad. For the first time in thirty years, my thoughts are clear. I can speak with good common sense. And

I shall continue to do so. But I think we have flown far enough away from that house of death, Hepzibah. We shall get off at the next stop and decide where to go from there."

A short time later, the two wanderers were standing on a deserted station platform, gazing around them. A distance away stood an old wooden church with broken windows and crumbling walls. A deserted farmhouse stood just beyond it in ruins.

The heavy wind was driving pouring rain against them. Clifford began to shiver from head to foot. The joy and enthusiasm he had been feeling on the train had completely vanished. The excitement that had given him his youthful energy was leaving him.

"You must lead me now, Hepzibah," he murmured weakly.

Hepzibah knelt down on the wet platform and lifted her hands to the heavens. "Oh, God!" she prayed. "Are we not Thy children? Have mercy on us!"

The Two Wanderers

CHAPTER 17

The Mystery of the Locked Mansion

While Hepzibah and Clifford were on the train, Judge Jaffrey was left sitting in that armchair, not stirring hand or foot, not moving his eyes from the watch in his hand, which by now had stopped ticking.

The judge had many appointments that day. Now it was already two hours that he had not moved from the chair. He was to see his broker; he was to attend a real-estate auction; he was to speak at a charity meeting; he was to buy some new peach trees for his fruit orchard; he was to see his doctor to see about the dizziness in his head and the choking and gurgling he often felt in his throat; and he was to attend a dinner where he was to be the guest of honor and probably be named his party's candidate for governor of the state in the next election.

Yes, Judge Jaffrey Pyncheon certainly was a busy man. But for hours, he hadn't moved in his chair in the study at Pyncheon House.

And so he sat, as day turned to night and night into morning. Nothing disturbed the old man, not even the fly that landed on his forehead, and then jumped onto his nose.

The silence was broken by the ringing of the shop's bell. Life had returned to The House of the Seven Gables. But could it wake the dead?

Only moments before the shop bell had rung, Uncle Venner had turned into Pyncheon Street on his regular morning rounds, looking into the trash people put aside for him, with which he fed his pig. He picked up discarded cabbage leaves, turnip tops and potato skins for the animal. Uncle Venner's pickups from Pyncheon House had greatly improved since Clifford returned and more cooking was being

"Good Morning, Uncle Venner."

done. So he was very disappointed when he found Hepzibah's large trash pail empty.

"I never knew Miss Hepzibah to be so forgetful before," he muttered. "She surely must have made dinner yesterday, so where can the leftovers be? Well, it's too early to disturb them now by ringing the bell, so I'll come back later."

As Uncle Venner was walking out the front gate, the sound of its creaking hinges reached an open window in Mr. Holgrave's gable.

"Good morning, Uncle Venner," the young man called. "Do you hear anyone awake?"

"Not a soul. But that's to be expected. Maybe the storm last night kept them awake. I can understand why Miss Hepzibah would oversleep this morning. But it would be odd, would it not, if the judge had taken Miss Hepzibah and Clifford to his country house? I saw him go into the shop yesterday."

"What time was that?" asked Holgrave.

"Oh, some time before noon," said the old man. "But I'll go along now and come back later for the scraps for my pig."

A while after Uncle Venner left, a housewife hurried up to the shop door and tried the handle. But the door was locked. She tried it again, this time with such force that the bell jingled.

"The devil take Old Maid Pyncheon!" she cried. "She sets up a shop, then stays in bed till noon. I guess it's her fancy airs. But I'll either wake up that high and mighty lady or break down the door!"

The woman angrily shook the door with all her might, and while the bell didn't wake the dead man in the study, the banging on the door woke the woman who lived across the street. She came to her window and called across, "There's nobody there, Mrs. Gubbins."

"There had better be!" replied Mrs. Gubbins. "I need some pork to fry the fish for Mr. Gubbins' breakfast. I don't care if Old Maid Pyncheon does consider herself a fancy lady, she'd better get up and open the shop for me!"

"Listen, Mrs. Gubbins," called out the lady at the window. "Yesterday, I saw Old Maid Pyncheon and her brother leaving in the storm. They must

But the Door Was Locked.

have gone with their cousin, the judge, to his country home. The only one in the house is that young photographer in the north gable."

Finally convinced that the shop was indeed closed, Mrs. Gubbins stormed off, muttering angrily at Hepzibah's absence.

For the next hour, Pyncheon Street was quiet until young Ned Higgins came trudging up the street on his way to school. With a penny in his pocket for the first time in two weeks, he was eagerly looking forward to a gingerbread treat. But in spite of all his banging on the shop door and the jiggling of the handle, the door wouldn't open.

Next, he tried rapping on the window. "Miss Pyncheon!" called the boy. "I want an elephant."

After several more raps and shouts, Ned picked up a stone, ready to fling it. His hand was stopped in midair by a passerby.

"Put down that stone and get along to school," said the man. Then turning to the friend he had been walking with, he said, "Dixie, I can't understand these Pyncheons.

First I hear from Smith the stableman that the judge left his horse at the stable yesterday morning for what was supposed to be only a few hours. But the judge never came back to pick up the animal. Then one of the judge's servants came to the stable this morning looking for him. I think we ought to go to the police."

"Oh, he'll turn up," answered Dixie. "But as far as that Old Maid Pyncheon, she's probably in such debt from that shop, she's run away from her creditors. Too many women are opening these shops and losing money, just like my wife did."

During the rest of the morning, several people tried to get into the shop, some to buy, others to deliver orders.

The butcher was very persistent with his delivery. He went around to every door to the house, ending at the door to the shop. The man was tall enough to see through the window in the door. No one was there, but he was able to see into part of the study through its open door.

"Now what's going on?" he muttered. "I

The Organ-Grinder and His Monkey

see someone in there. At least I see a pair of black trousers. It seems as if someone is sitting in that large armchair, but I can't see the rest of the person. The chair is turned the other way. The back of it is blocking my view. Well, if someone's there and won't answer, they're losing out on a good piece of meat! It's probably Old Maid Pyncheon's invisible brother ignoring me completely. I'll have none of this! I'm leaving!" He tossed his bundle of meat back in his cart and drove off in a huff.

A while later, the organ-grinder and his monkey stopped under the Pyncheon Elm. They were soon followed by a mob of children. The smiling face of Phoebe, and the coins she always threw down so generously had been bringing the musician back to this spot very often.

The organ-grinder kept playing until two men passing by interrupted him.

"Come away from there!" one of the men called. "The Pyncheons are in great trouble! It is reported all over town that Judge Pyncheon has been murdered and the police are going to investigate. So, you'd better leave right away!"

As the organ-grinder was packing up to leave, he spotted a card on the doorstep. He picked it up and handed it to the man who had just sent him away.

The man, Dixie, who had passed by earlier, looked at the card. "See the fancy gold engraving with Judge Jaffrey Pyncheon's name," he said to the other man. "And look at the back. He must have written notes to remind himself of his appointments for the day. This card is soaking wet. It's probably been out here since before last night's storm."

"We'd better go to the police with the card," said Dixie's friend. "Suppose the judge went into that door and never came out again. Suppose his cousin Clifford was up to his murderous old tricks again. And suppose Old Maid Pyncheon, being in such debt, and the judge's pockets so full of money—well, see what I'm getting at?"

"Hush! Not so loud!" Dixie whispered.

"You'd Better Leave!"

"But I agree. We must go to the police!"

The remaining children scattered after overhearing Dixie and his friend talking. For the rest of the day people took another street to get where they were going, while a few of the children showed off their courage by challenging each other to race past The House of the Seven Gables at full speed.

Some time later, a coach drove down Pyncheon Street and stopped beneath the Pyncheon Elm. A coachman took several trunks and bags from the top, then helped Phoebe down to the ground.

Phoebe first tried the shop door. Then she hurried to the front door of the house. She knocked and knocked again, then a third time. Her only answer was silence.

Phoebe then went around back into the garden. Perhaps Clifford and Hepzibah are there on this sunny day, she thought.

But Phoebe was greeted only by the family of hens. "Oh, well," she said with a sigh, "I guess my cousins are just keeping to themselves inside the house."

Phoebe headed for the back door from the garden. It too was locked. She knocked once. The door was immediately opened, but only part-way. That was how Hepzibah had always opened the door.

Phoebe stepped inside the darkened hallway. The door was instantly closed by someone behind her!

A Hand Grasped Hers.

CHAPTER 18

Love Blooms

Coming from the bright sunshine into the darkened house, Phoebe was blinded for an instant and wasn't certain who had let her in. Before her eyes could become accustomed to the darkness, a hand grasped hers, and led her through the hallway. They weren't headed into the study but rather to another unoccupied room in the house.

The sunshine in this room revealed that it was Holgrave whose warm hand held hers. Phoebe had no wish to pull away. Still, she sensed that something was wrong in the house, and she looked eagerly into Holgrave's face,

217

questioning him with her eyes.

Holgrave looked pale, but his smile for Phoebe was full of warmth. But it quickly faded when he had to answer Phoebe's questioning look.

"Phoebe," he began, "I am overjoyed that you have returned—but this is a terrible time."

"Why? What has happened?" she asked fearfully. "Where are Clifford and Hepzibah?"

"Gone! And I have no idea where."

"My cousins gone? It is not possible! And why have you brought me into this room and not into the study? I fear something terrible has happened. Let me go and see!"

"No! No, Phoebe, don't!" Holgrave stopped her. "They are gone, it's true. You are correct— something terrible has happened. But not to them, and not because of them."

"Then what?"

"Phoebe, dear," Holgrave whispered, "you are gentle, yet strong and wise. I am certain you will deal with this situation, and I depend on you to tell me what to do."

"Something Terrible Has Happened."

"Strong?   No—I am weak," Phoebe replied, and her soft voice was trembling. " M r. Holgrave, you must tell me what has happened. Tell me! Not knowing is terrifying me!"

Holgrave hesitated, reluctant to tell this sweet innocent girl the awful secret in the study. But she had to know.

"Phoebe, remember when I showed you this portrait?"

"Yes, but what has this to do with Clifford and Hepzibah?" she asked, impatient that Holgrave should be discussing daguerreotypes with her now. "It is Judge Pyncheon. I saw it already."

"And here's the same face I took a half-hour ago. I was just developing it when you knocked at the door," Holgrave told her quietly.

"But this is a picture of Judge Pyncheon dead!" cried Phoebe, turning pale.

"Yes, Phoebe, he sits in the study, dead," Holgrave said. "Clifford and Hepzibah are gone. When I came home last night, there were no lights in the house and no sound of any movement in the house, either. This morning I heard a neighbor say she saw them leave the house during yesterday's storm."

"Why would they go out in a storm?" Phoebe wondered aloud.

"I have no idea, Phoebe, but early today, I heard a rumor that Judge Pyncheon was missing. A feeling came over me telling me to come to this part of the house. I unlocked the door separating my gable from theirs, and discovered the judge dead in a chair in the study."

Holgrave was calm. He seemed not too surprised at the judge's death, perhaps because of the Pyncheon history of murder and mystery.

"But why haven't you called the police?" asked Phoebe. "And why didn't you open the door to let anyone in as a witness? It must have been terrible to be here all alone!"

"I'm concerned about Clifford and Hepzibah, not about my being alone with a corpse. We have to think of what's best for your two poor cousins. The fact that they have run away will make it appear they are guilty of harming the judge. After all, the situation

"No Good Can Come of It."

is so similar to the one that sent Clifford to prison. If Hepzibah had called for help and if Clifford had opened the door to let people in, it would have looked better for them, perhaps even helped to remove the black stain on Clifford's reputation."

"Oh, this is so dreadful!" Phoebe sobbed. "No good can come of it."

"That is not so, Phoebe. If they had been here, perhaps it could finally explain how these strange deaths have happened throughout the Pyncheon family. The legend of Old Maule's curse probably began with people who knew the Pyncheon family over the years. This is the same way Clifford's uncle died thirty years ago. But I have reason to suspect that the uncle, old Jaffrey Pyncheon, was not murdered."

"But how? And by whom?" Phoebe asked.

"Clifford would never murder anyone!" said Phoebe.

"I have believed for a long time that the older Jaffrey died a natural death. But before it was made public, someone made it seem like murder by planting evidence to point to

Clifford as the murderer," Holgrave continued.

"But who would do that to poor Clifford?" Phoebe wailed.

Holgrave pointed to the study. "The evil man who sits dead in the chair inside that room. Judge Jaffrey Pyncheon. But now, somehow this evil man has been punished for his wickedness."

"Then we must open the doors and let everyone know what has happened," Phoebe said. "They will see the truth. And you, dear Mr. Holgrave, how terrible it must have been for you to have found him!" she said again.

"What happened, dear Phoebe, was that about an hour before you arrived, I realized I was living in a world of darkness and evil. But then you came back and brought joy back with you. I must confess, Phoebe, I love you."

"I am only a simple country girl. I could not make you happy," Phoebe protested. "You are so wise, you have traveled, you are—"

"Dear Phoebe," Holgrave interrupted, "you are my only hope for happiness. Do you love me?"

"You Brought Joy Back with You."

"Look into my heart, dear friend," she said shyly. "You can see I love you."

It was at this moment that the miracle of love and a sweet kiss made the two young people forget the dead man in the next room.

"Listen," Phoebe whispered. "Someone is at the front door!"

"Then we shall meet the world," said Holgrave. "Surely the rumor of Jaffrey Pyncheon's visit here and the escape of Clifford and Hepzibah will lead to an investigation of this house. We shall meet the situation now. We shall meet it together!"

But before they could reach the front door to open it, they heard footsteps in the hallway. The door, which everyone had found locked, had been opened from the outside. The footsteps they heard were not the hard, loud sounds one would expect from the police. They were slow and weak, and the murmuring voices were familiar ones.

"Can it be?" Holgrave whispered.

"It is Clifford and Hepzibah!" Phoebe

exclaimed. "Thank God!"

Then they heard Hepzibah's voice moaning, "Thank God, my brother, we are home!"

"Yes, thank God!" Clifford answered. "But I cannot walk past that open study door. I'll go rest in the garden where I have spent so many happy hours with little Phoebe."

But the two old people hadn't taken another step when Phoebe ran into the hallway to greet them. Hepzibah burst into tears and hugged the girl.

Clifford shook Holgrave's hand. "It is our little Phoebe and Holgrave with her!" he said joyfully. "And I'm certainly not too old that I can't see love in the eyes of two young people!"

The Death of the Judge Caused a Stir.

CHAPTER 19

A Murderous Past Is Revealed!

The sudden death of such an important person as the Honorable Judge Jaffrey Pyncheon created a stir in the town for the next two weeks. Certainly the way he died might have held the public's curiosity longer if he had been murdered. But when police and government officials declared that the death was natural, caused by a stroke, the public soon forgot that Jaffrey Pyncheon had ever lived.

However, those who had been touched by the judge's evil hand during his lifetime continued to talk about him, especially about the events surrounding the death of his and

Clifford's uncle, Old Jaffrey Pyncheon, thirty years before.

Old Jaffrey Pyncheon had spent his last moments in his private apartment. It was said that someone had entered and ransacked his desk and drawers. Money and valuable treasures were missing from the room. The police began to suspect that the person guilty of the robbery and murder was Clifford, who had been living in The House of the Seven Gables with his uncle, old Jaffrey.

Now, years later, a new theory arose as to that murder, a theory that did not involve Clifford. It was said that the facts leading to this new theory were discovered under hypnosis, and were told to Holgrave.

Judge Pyncheon, as a young man, had been wild. He drank heavily and cared only for his own pleasures, which he paid for with his uncle's money. Uncle Jaffrey was a bachelor and had treated young Jaffrey like a son. Then the old man got tired of his nephew Jaffrey's wicked and dishonest lifestyle and stopped sup-

Valuable Treasures Were Missing.

porting him.

One night, young Jaffrey sneaked into his uncle's room and was searching through his uncle's private papers when the old man opened the door to his room and caught him. The shock of being betrayed by his nephew Jaffrey caused the old man to have a stroke. Blood gurgled in his throat and choked him. As he fell to the floor he struck his head against the corner of the desk and appeared dead.

Young Jaffrey did not seek help for his uncle. He feared that if the old man had lived, he would remember what Jaffrey had done. So Jaffrey paid no attention to his dying uncle and continued searching the old man's papers. Among those papers was a recent will. Uncle Jaffrey was leaving his estate to Clifford! Jaffrey destroyed this will and put in its place an earlier one that left the Pyncheon fortune to him.

Jaffrey also had to make certain that he would not be suspected of robbery and murder, so he decided to frame Clifford—to make Clifford look like the guilty one. Jaffrey had always looked down upon Clifford's fine, honest, upstanding lifestyle.

So, at Clifford's trial, Jaffrey concealed what he had done, and was silent about what he had witnessed of his uncle's death. He gave little thought to the evil deeds of his past as he went on to become the Honorable Judge Pyncheon.

Now, shortly after the judge's death, word came that his only son, who had been leading a bad life in Europe, had died there from cholera. As a result, all the Pyncheon land and fortune was inherited by Clifford, Hepzibah and Phoebe. And, of course, through Phoebe now to her husband-to-be, Mr. Holgrave as well.

By now, it was too late for Clifford to clear himself in a court. But he didn't care. He wanted only the love of a few people in his life, not the admiration or respect of townspeople.

The shock of Judge Pyncheon's death seemed to have a strengthening effect on Clifford. It lifted the nightmare out of his life and brought him close to his old self. Even

They Gathered in the Study.

when he quieted down, Clifford didn't sink into his old mental depression. He recovered enough to behave almost normally and began to be truly happy in his new life.

Very soon after inheriting the Pyncheon wealth, Clifford, Hepzibah and Phoebe moved from the dismal House of the Seven Gables to the elegant country house of the late Judge Pyncheon, which was now theirs.

On the day of their departure, the family gathered in the study, along with Holgrave and Uncle Venner.

"This house has inherited so much misfortune, I'll be happy to leave it," said Clifford, "and especially to get out from under the eye of the evil colonel in that portrait!"

But even as Clifford looked at the portrait, he seemed to shrink back in his chair as if to shrink back from his old ancestor.

"Whenever I look at it, I seem to be haunted by a memory, almost a dream," he gasped. "It had something to do with wealth, unimaginable wealth! I remember that when I was a child, I thought the portrait spoke to me and told me a secret. It held out a document that described the secret. But those memories are so dim now. I don't know if they were real, or a childish fantasy."

"Perhaps I can help you recall," said Holgrave, walking toward the portrait. "See, it is highly unlikely that anyone who didn't know the secret would ever touch this spring." And he pointed to a small mechanism in the picture frame.

"A secret spring!" cried Clifford. "Yes, I remember now! I discovered it one summer afternoon when I was idling here in the parlor long, long ago. But I still can't figure out the mystery."

Holgrave put his finger on the small spring. "Two hundred years ago," he explained, "the spring would have caused the portrait to move forward. But the mechanism has rusted over the years."

As Holgrave pressed on the spring, the portrait fell and revealed a secret recess—a

The Portrait Fell.

hiding place—in the wall. Inside, covered with two hundred years of dust, was a rolled piece of parchment paper.

Holgrave opened the parchment carefully and explained, "This is an ancient deed to the vast Eastern Lands once owned by its native people, the Indians. It transferred the lands to Colonel Pyncheon and his heirs forever, and was signed with symbols of the tribal chiefs.

"The struggle among the Pyncheons and the Maules to find this very parchment caused the death of the beautiful Alice Pyncheon," said Holgrave. "The deed is what all the Pyncheons have been looking for, over all these years. And now that it is found, it is worthless, because all that land has been divided up and belongs to hundreds of different people."

"Poor Cousin Jaffrey!" Hepzibah said. "This is what deceived him. When they were very young, Clifford was always dreaming up stories about the house and its secrets. Poor Jaffrey believed all these fanciful tales and thought that Clifford knew where our uncle's wealth was hidden."

Phoebe turned to Holgrave. "How did you learn about the secret?"

"My dearest Phoebe, my wife-to-be," said Holgrave gently, "would you be very troubled for your married name to be Maule? The secret of that deed is the only inheritance I have from my Maule ancestors. I wanted to tell you sooner, but I didn't want to frighten you away. I did not want you to think that I was a wizard like my ancestor, Matthew Maule. Actually, when this house was being built by Thomas Maule, Matthew's son, he built that recess in the wall for the colonel. Who hid the deed in it remains a mystery to this day, but it was the deed Pyncheon needed to trade Maule for the land that this house and garden were built on."

Uncle Venner chuckled. "And now the claim to that land isn't worth one man's share in my retirement farm!"

"Oh, Uncle Venner," Phoebe laughed, taking the wise old man's hand. "You shall never go to the poorhouse—as long as you live! There is a pretty cottage in our new garden, which shall be yours! You can bring your pig too. He'll keep Chanticleer and his family company. You and Cousin Clifford can spend many happy hours together in pleasant conversation."

At that moment, a fine carriage drew up in front of The House of the Seven Gables. Everyone left the mansion. Clifford and Hepzibah turned back for one last look at Pyncheon House, but they felt nothing—just relief.

A group of children had gathered around the carriage, and Hepzibah recognized little Ned Higgins among them. She reached into her purse and handed her first and most loyal customer enough silver coins to buy a whole parade of gingerbread animal cookies.

Hepzibah and Clifford had entered the bright sunshine of the outside world. Phoebe and Holgrave had joined together to break the curse of the two families and unite the Pyncheons and Maules... far away from the bleakness of The House of the Seven Gables!